D0562443

It was nearly three weeks after his encounter with Mouchette when the shot came. Preacher was gathering his first crop of beaver pelt. The traps were full, and the beaver were prime with rich coats. He had just bent over to check something when a ball whizzed by, right where his head had been. Had the shot been fired half a second earlier, Preacher's blood and brains would have decorated the tree beside him. Instead, there was just a streak of green wood in the tree where the bullet had chewed off a limb and stripped away some of the bark.

Preacher dove to the ground, burrowed into the snow, and turned to look in the direction from which the shot had come. Just below a snow-bearing pine bough, he saw a puff of smoke hanging in the cold, still air.

Wriggling through the snow on his belly, Preacher returned to his kit. Grabbing his rifle, he rolled onto his back and began loading it. He poured powder into the barrel, then used his ramrod to tamp the wad down. All the while he was loading his rifle, he kept his eyes toward the tree line. He knew that whoever shot at him would also be reloading, and his assailant had a head start.

# WILLIAM W. JOHNSTONE

## THE FIRST MOUNTAIN MAN:
# PREACHER'S JUSTICE

**PINNACLE BOOKS**
Kensington Publishing Corp.
http://www.kensingtonbooks.com

PINNACLE BOOKS are published by

Kensington Publishing Corp.
119 West 40th Street
New York, NY 10018

Copyright © 2004 by William W. Johnstone

All rights reserved. No part of this book may be reproduced in any form or by any means without the prior written consent of the Publisher, excepting brief quotes used in reviews.

If you purchased this book without a cover, you should be aware that this book is stolen property. It was reported as "unsold and destroyed" to the Publisher and neither the Author nor the Publisher has received any payment for this "stripped book."

This novel is a work of fiction. Names, characters, places, and incidents are either the product of the author's imagination, or are used fictitiously. Any resemblace to actual persons, living or dead, or events is entirely coincidental.

All Kensington Titles, Imprints, and Distributed Lines are available at special quantity discounts for bulk purchases for sales promotion, premiums, fund-raising, and educational, or institutional use. Special book excerpts or customized printings can also be created to fit specific needs. For details, write or phone the office of the Kensington special sales manager: Kensington Publishing Corp., 119 West 40th Street, New York, NY 10018. attn. Special Sales Department. Phone: 1-800-221-2647.

Pinnacle and the P logo Reg. U.S. Pat. & TM Off.

ISBN-13: 978-0-7860-3276-1
ISBN-10: 0-7860-3276-6

First Pinnacle Books Printing: January 2004

20  19  18  17  16  15  14  13  12  11  10

Printed in the United States of America

# ONE

The sky over the Rocky Mountains was a brilliant, crystalline blue. Though it was cloudless now, it had snowed steadily for the previous twenty-four hours and a deep pack on the ground was painfully bright under the relentless sun. It also made traveling difficult, so the man everyone called Preacher had not even attempted to ride his horse this morning. Instead, the mountain man and fur trapper had taken a pack mule with him, and he led the animal, laboriously breaking a path through the nearly waist-deep snow. The mule was carrying a string of beaver traps that, over the previous several days, had been carefully inspected. Repairs had been made as necessary.

Preacher, who was twenty-seven years old, had been trapping in these mountains since he was fourteen. He had a dark shock of hair that he kept trimmed with a sharp knife. Though it was sometimes difficult to do so, he also managed to shave at least two or three times a week so that, while he often had stubble, he never had a beard. His eyes were dark. From a distance one might think they were brown, but upon closer examination they proved to be a deep, cobalt blue. He was a little taller than average, and slender of build, but with broad shoulders and muscular arms and powerful legs strengthened by his years of trapping in the mountains.

Preacher looked toward a distinctive peak and saw feathery tendrils of snow streaming out from it in the cold, piercing wind of the higher climes. The snow crystals glistened in the sun and formed a prism of color to crown the beauty of the rugged mountains and dark green trees. From that peak, which Preacher called Eagle's Beak, the young mountain man got his bearings. Thus oriented, he started up a narrow draw until he found the creek he was looking for.

Preacher ground-hobbled his mule, took some of the traps, then stepped out into the stream, breaking through the thin ice that had formed at the stream's edge. The nearly paralyzing cold shot up his legs as he waded in the water, looking for the best place to put his traps. It would have been easier and less painful to move along the shoreline, but he'd learned long ago to use the water as a means of masking his scent from the beaver.

Finally, he came to the place he had discovered five years earlier, a place rich with beaver that had so far, been undiscovered by the other trappers. Since his discovery, he had worked this area as if it were his own private reserve. While there was no such thing as privately owned land here, the trappers recognized and followed a code of the right of territory according to who came first.

Dropping all his traps in the water, Preacher began setting them by depressing the springs by standing on them, putting one foot on each trap arm to open it up. When the trap was opened, he engaged the pan notch, holding it in the set position.

As each trap was set, he would extend the trap chain to its fullest length out toward the deeper water, where a trap stake was passed through the ring at the end of the chain and driven into the stream bed.

Finally, he placed the bait. The bait was a wand of willow, cut to a length that would permit its small end to extend from the stream bank directly over the pan of the trap. Bark was scraped from the stick and castoreum was smeared on the end of the switch, so that it hung about six inches or more above the trap. Castoreum was an oil taken from the glands of a beaver. Once his traps were set, Preacher returned to the tiny cabin he would call home while wintering in the mountains.

It was no secret that Preacher had hit upon a mother lode of beaver. Every year his catch was consistently the highest, or very near the highest, taken. While others might have envied him his good luck, they were bound by the code they all followed not to horn in on him.

But there was one trapper who wasn't bound by this, or any other code, and he was determined to find Preacher's secret location. He didn't know where Preacher trapped, but he did know where he lived. He had made camp near Preacher's cabin, surviving the storm just passed, in order to follow him to his secret place.

The recent snow made it very easy to follow, because he didn't even have to stay in contact with Preacher. All he had to do was follow the path left by Preacher and his mule through the snow.

"It'll be like taking a sugar-tit from a baby," he said with a gruff laugh.

His traps set, Preacher returned to his little cabin. This was his seventh year in this same location, and over the years he had made several modifications to improve the living conditions. The thick log walls were well chinked with mud and insulated with moss so that even the coldest arctic blasts were kept at bay.

Initially, the cabin had been heated with a fire-place, but a few years ago he'd bought an iron stove at Rendezvous and hauled it back on one of his pack mules. The stove was a marvel of efficiency, heating the cabin much better and with considerably less wood than was consumed by the fireplace. It also made it easier to cook his meals because he could set a pot right on top of the stove, rather than moving it from place to place within the fireplace.

Preacher had become a pretty good cook over the years of living alone. When he returned home after setting the traps, he was greeted with the enticing aroma of a simmering beaver-tail stew. He rolled out some biscuits and put them on to bake.

Automatically, he made an extra biscuit for Dog, then remembered that Dog wasn't with him. Dog was back in St. Louis, looking after Jennie.

Preacher missed the animal that had been his sole companion out here. He recalled the way he had come by Dog. A few years ago, the traders at Rendezvous had formed an alliance designed to keep the price of pelts down. Preacher had decided to take his pelts back to St. Louis and sell them himself.

He was about three weeks on the trail when shortly after nightfall, as he was laying out his bedroll, he became aware of eyes staring at him from the dark. With the hair standing up on the back of his neck, he slipped his pistol from his belt and stared into the black maw that surrounded his camp.

"Who's there?" he called.

There was no response.

"Who's there?" he called again, and this time he augmented his call with the deadly clicking sound of his pistol being cocked.

A low, frightening growl came from the darkness.

"Are you a wolf?" Preacher called.

Thinking to lure the animal from the darkness, he took a piece of rabbit and held it up. "Come on in, boy. Come get this meat."

Tossing the meat about ten feet in front of him,

he raised his pistol, ready to shoot the moment the wolf showed itself.

It wasn't a wolf, at least not a full-blooded wolf, though it clearly had many of the markings and features of a wolf. It was a dog. The animal walked into pistol range, growling, its eyes locked on the mountain man as it moved toward the proffered morsel.

Preacher lowered his pistol and watched as the big dog used its powerful jaws to pull the meat away from the bone. The dog fascinated him, not only by its size and power, but also by the way it carried itself, clearly showing no fear.

When the dog finished the first piece of meat, Preacher threw another piece out, this one closer to him than the first. The dog came for it. By the time he threw the last piece of meat, the dog was quite close. In fact, it was close enough for Preacher to touch. He did so, rubbing the dog behind its ears.

"How'd you get way out here in the middle of nowhere?" Preacher asked.

Though the dog didn't snuggle against his hand, it was friendly enough to be non-threatening. The growling had ceased.

The dog slept near Preacher that night, and when Preacher got ready to leave the next day, the dog jumped onto the boat with him. Preacher named the dog "Dog," and they became companions. Preacher always thought of him as his companion, not as his possession. Dog clearly belonged to no one but Dog.

Last year, concerned for the safety of Jennie, he left Dog with her, charging the animal with the responsibility of looking out for the woman that came closer to being Preacher's woman than any other. Thus it was that when Preacher returned to the mountains, Dog went with Jennie to St. Louis.

Clearly, Dog would have preferred to come back with Preacher. It showed in his eyes as Preacher took his leave. But Preacher had made it personal, asking Dog, as a favor to him, to stay and watch after Jennie. Dog accepted the responsibility without complaint.

"I miss you, Dog," Preacher said aloud. "I can get along without people just fine. Truth to tell, I prefer it without people. But I do wish I had you around to keep me company."

It wasn't all that unusual for Preacher to talk aloud, even though there was no one there. Although he enjoyed solitude, there were times when he wanted to hear a human voice, even if it was his own.

When the biscuits were done, Preacher took a couple of them, spooned up a generous serving of the stew, and sat at the crude table he had made to enjoy his dinner.

As Preacher ate his meal, he went through the figures in his little ledger book. If he had as good a year this year as he did last, and he had no reason to suspect that he wouldn't, he would be able to add substantially to his bank account.

By the standards of the day, Preacher could almost count himself a rich man. He was worth just under fifteen thousand dollars, and would go over that amount by the end of the season. The funny thing was, money meant nothing to him except as a means of keeping score. With what he had now, he could buy the finest house in St. Louis and live in luxury for many years.

Sometimes he felt guilty for not doing that. He could marry Jennie and make a good life for her and for himself. But even the thought of such a thing was difficult to consider. He looked up from his ledger and peeked through the window—made of real glass that he'd packed in three years ago—at the ruggedly beautiful terrain surrounding his cabin.

"I'm sorry, Jennie, ole girl," Preacher said quietly. "To the degree that I can understand love between a man and a woman, I probably love you. But if I gave all this up, I would have such a hunger for it in my heart that there would be nothing left for you. I hope you understand."

When Preacher returned to check out his traps a few days later, he was surprised to see that they had all been removed, set aside, and replaced by another man's traps. Angrily, he removed the new traps and put his own back in place. The process took most of the day.

It was one thing to crowd in on another man's territory. That was done from time to time, and it nearly always brought about harsh feelings. But to actually remove another man's traps was an affront of the worst kind.

Preacher considered breaking the offending traps, but finally decided against it. Instead, he left one of them on the bank of the stream and placed rocks on the ground in the form of an arrow, pointing toward his cabin, indicating that if the man wanted to retrieve his traps, he would have to come see Preacher to get them. When Preacher returned to his cabin, he hung the poacher's traps up on the outside wall, in plain view of anyone who might happen by.

Exactly one week later, Preacher was tending to his mules when he saw a lone figure trekking across the snowcovered meadow that separated Preacher's cabin from the woods. The man was wearing a buffalo robe and a fur cap, and as he crossed the meadow he left a long, dark smear in the pristine white snow behind him.

No doubt, this was the one who had attempted to poach on Preacher's territory. Preacher had left his weapons inside. However, there was a hatchet nearby. Preacher felt a sense of security in believing that if need be, he could arm himself.

Before the man was halfway across the meadow, Preacher recognized him as Henri Mouchette. He wasn't surprised that this was the man who had so blatantly violated the trappers' code. Mouchette had the reputation of being someone who was very hard to get along with. He was even suspected of stealing from other traps, though as no one had ever actually caught him doing it, the accusation had never been brought before the trappers' court.

"Hello, Mouchette," Preacher greeted him. "What brings you by?" Preacher knew full well why Mouchette was there, but he decided to play the game.

Mouchette stopped a few feet away from Preacher. He was breathing rather hard from the effort of both climbing and having to cut a trail through the snow. Clouds of vapor surrounded his head.

"You son of a bitch, you stole my traps," Mouchette said.

"I haven't stolen them, Mouchette," Preacher replied. He pointed to the traps hanging from his front wall. "As you can see, they are hanging right here, in clear sight."

"They're here now, but you took them from the stream," Mouchette said.

"Oh, yes, siree, I did that, all right," Preacher said easily. "As a matter of fact, I took them right after you took mine."

"That is my place," Mouchette insisted, pointing to himself with his thumb.

"And what makes you think that is your place, seein' as I was there first?" Preacher asked.

"I been trappin' that stream for years. Hell, I was trappin' it when you was a pup," Mouchette said.

"You know as well as I do that the first person to arrive at a stream has the right to put out his own traps. I didn't see any traps here when I arrived."

"I laid off a couple of years because I didn't want the stream to be over-trapped," Mouchette said. "I quit trapping so it could recover. Then, when I went back to it, I seen your traps there. I didn't figure that to be right, so I took 'em out."

"Are you saying you were trapping there two years ago?" Preacher asked.

"Yeah, that's what I'm saying. Two years ago, I trapped the stream. Then I let it be for two years."

"Well, now, that's where the mistake is," Preacher said. "You must have your streams mixed up. I have been trapping this same stream for five years now, so you couldn't have been here two years ago."

"I ain't the one that made the mistake. It was you," Mouchette insisted. "By all that's right, that stream belongs to me."

"Not now, it doesn't. Put your traps somewhere else."

"I aim to put my traps right back where I had them," Mouchette insisted. "And I plan to get your traps out of there."

Preacher's eyes narrowed. "Well now, Mr. Mouchette, I would strongly advise you against doing that," he said.

Mouchette glared at Preacher for a long moment. Then, without another word, he took his traps and trekked back into the woods, once more leaving his footprints in the snow behind him. Preacher noted, with some satisfaction, that he wasn't heading toward the stream in question.

Preacher waited four days before he returned to the stream. Evidently, Mouchette had paid heed to Preacher's warning, because Preacher's traps were still in place.

* * *

It was nearly three weeks after his encounter with Mouchette when the shot came. Preacher was gathering his first crop of beaver pelt. The traps were full, and the beaver were prime with rich coats. He had bent over to check something when a ball whizzed by, right where his head had been. Had the shot been fired half a second earlier, Preacher's blood and brains would have decorated the tree beside him. Instead, there was just a streak of green wood in the tree where the bullet had chewed off a limb and stripped away some of the bark.

Preacher dove to the ground, burrowed into the snow, and turned to look in the direction from which the shot had come. Just below a snow-bearing pine bough, he saw a puff of smoke hanging in the cold, still air. This was where the shot had come from.

Wriggling through the snow on his belly, Preacher returned to his kit. Grabbing his rifle, he rolled onto his back and began loading it. He poured powder into the barrel, then used his ramrod to tamp the wad down. All the while he was loading his rifle, he kept his eyes toward the tree line from which the shot had come. He knew that whoever shot at him would also be reloading, and his assailant had a head start.

Just as Preacher was dropping in the ball, he saw a rifle barrel protrude from the trees, not where the smoke of the first shot was, but from some distance away. His assailant had cleverly changed positions after the first shot.

Preacher rolled hard to the right, just as a flash of fire erupted from the end of the protruding rifle barrel. The ball crashed into the snow where Preacher had been.

"Now, you son of a bitch! You're empty and I'm loaded," Preacher said. Standing, he moved quickly toward the puff of smoke.

But Preacher had miscalculated, because another barrel suddenly appeared, not a rifle, but a pistol. Preacher realized, too late, that his assailant had loaded his pistol as well and was holding it in reserve.

Once again, Preacher had to throw himself to the ground in order to avoid being shot, and once again, the ball came so close to him that he could hear it whizzing by his ear. When Preacher hit the ground this time, he felt himself tumbling, slipping, and sliding down the side of a long hill. When he finally stopped, he was more than one hundred feet below where he started.

Scrambling back to his feet, Preacher searched through the snow until he found his rifle. Cleaning the flint and pan of snow, he worked his way back up the hill. When he got to the top, he started toward the tree line where he had last seen his assailant. He found marks in the snow where the man had waited in ambush for him, but whoever it was had gone.

Following the trail the assailant left, Preacher saw someone hurrying across an open field, trying to reach the safety of the woods on the other side. He was too far away for Preacher to be certain, but there was something about the way the man was moving that made Preacher believe it was Mouchette. And of course, as he thought about it, Mouchette was the only one who would have a motive to attack him now.

Preacher raised the rifle to his shoulder and aimed. Mouchette, if that was who it was, was just on the extreme outer range of his rifle. Despite the great range, Preacher was an exceptionally good shot. He knew that if he pulled the trigger, there was a good chance he would hit him.

Preacher took a breath, let half of it out, then gradually began to increase the pressure on the trigger. Then, taking his finger off the trigger, he sighed and lowered the rifle. Whoever it was had tried to kill him, and he had every right to shoot. But Preacher's life wasn't in immediate danger right now. To shoot a man in the back, while he was fleeing, didn't set well with Preacher—even though that man had tried to kill him.

Raising the rifle to his shoulder again, he aimed—not to kill, but to frighten. He squeezed the trigger. The rifle boomed and rocked him back, a cloud of smoke puffing up around him. He saw the strike of the ball in the snow, just a few feet in front of the fleeing man, and he saw the fleeing man throw himself to the ground in terror.

Preacher laughed. "Let that be a lesson to you, Mouchette," he said, positive now that Mouchette was the one who had attacked him. "If you come back, don't think you are going to get another shot at me."

Returning to work his trap line, Preacher leaned the rifle against a tree, then loaded his pistol and put it on the ground close by. Keeping both firearms loaded and ready, he went back to work.

"Damn, Dog, this is one time I could've really used you," he said, speaking aloud. "You would never have let anyone sneak up on me like that."

# TWO

*St. Louis*

Dog lay on the front porch of the little store into which Jennie had gone. There were some buildings he could go into, and some that he could not. Dog never understood exactly why it was like that, but he was aware of the difference, and he knew that this was one of those buildings where he was not welcome.

Being denied entry into a building didn't present a problem to Dog. Whenever he encountered a building in which he wasn't welcome, he would simply wait outside until Jennie came out again. He didn't care that much about being around many humans anyway.

Dog missed the life he had led before coming to this place. Part wolf, he was completely at home in the woods and the mountains. But he was part dog as well, and the part of him that was dog felt some primordial instinct to bond with man. The man Dog chose was well worthy of his bonding. For Dog had seen the man fight a bear and kill him. Others called that man Preacher, but Dog thought of him as Bear Killer.

Dog not only bonded with Bear Killer, but traveled with him as well. In their travels, they wound up here, in this place of many men and few animals. Dog had waited patiently for Bear Killer to leave this place of many men and few animals so he could return to the woods and the mountains.

Before it was time to leave, however, Bear Killer gave Dog a job to do. That job was to look after Bear Killer's woman. Dog wanted to leave with Bear Killer, but the part of him that was dog would not let him do so. Loyalty was the strongest trait of a dog, and Dog's loyalty was particularly well developed.

Others came and left the little store, but Bear Killer's woman, Jennie, was still inside. Dog slept on the porch, with his nose between his paws. As he slept, he dreamed of the woods and the mountains, of clear, sweet streams of water, and of rabbits he would chase down and eat. Yet, even as he was dreaming, a part of him was still alert. He assessed all who entered or left the store to determine whether or not they represented any danger to the woman he had been ordered to protect. Some would speak to him, others would go out of their way to avoid him, frightened by his powerful, wolf-like appearance. Dog actually preferred those who went out of their way to avoid him.

"There you are, Dog, right where I left you," Jennie said, coming out of the store. She squatted down beside him and smiled at him. Jennie was an exceptionally pretty woman with a smooth, olive-complexioned skin, high cheekbones, flashing brown eyes, and dark hair that hung in easy curls about her shoulders. She held a piece of ribbon beside her face. "Do you think this is pretty?" she asked.

Dog raised his head, then twisted it slightly, as if trying to respond to her question.

Jennie laughed. "Of course you think it's pretty. You're a good dog and you like anything I like. Come, let's go."

Jennie stepped down from the porch and Dog stood up, shook himself, then started after her.

*Philadelphia*

Theodore Epson sat across the desk from Joel Fontaine, the president of the Trust Bank of Philadelphia. They were in Fontaine's office, and as a measure of the size of the Trust Bank, Fontaine's office alone was as large the entire River Bank of St. Louis, the bank where Epson had worked before coming to Philadelphia.

"Mr. Epson, I have recently come in receipt of a very disturbing letter," Fontaine said, holding the letter up for Epson to see.

"A disturbing letter, sir? What type of letter?" Epson asked.

"It is a letter from one William Ashley of St.

Louis. I'm sure you are familiar with William Ashley, are you not?"

Epson began to get a little nervous, and a small line of sweat beaded on his upper lip. He took a handkerchief from his pocket and dabbed at it.

"Uh, yes, sir, indeed I do know Mr. Ashley," Epson said. He knew that whatever Ashley had to say in the letter about him couldn't be good. "Mr. Ashley is a furrier," Epson continued. "And as such, he is a man who must deal with the most common class of people. Unfortunately, I'm afraid he is sometimes unduly swayed by them."

"Unduly swayed by them?"

"Prone to believe them over the more substantial and trustworthy citizens of the community," Epson said.

"An interesting observation," Fontaine said, stroking his chin.

"I would be interested in hearing what Mr. Ashley has to say. What is the subject of the letter, if you don't mind sharing?"

"I don't mind sharing at all, as it concerns you."

"The letter concerns me? How so?"

"According to William Ashley, there was an incident in St. Louis where mortgage money duly paid to the River Bank of St. Louis was not credited."

"Well, now, I don't understand that," Epson said, nervously patting his mouth with his handkerchief. "Why would Mr. Ashley be writing to you about some business that supposedly took place in St. Louis? It would seem to me that he would take that up with the River Bank. And as I am no longer with the River Bank, why would that information, if it is true, concern me?"

Joel Fontaine cleared his throat. "Well, it has to do with you, Mr. Epson, because I'm afraid Mr. Ashley is accusing you of fraud."

"Me?" Epson said. "This is preposterous. I have no idea what you are even talking about. My record at the River Bank of St. Louis is spotless. Why, you checked my credentials yourself. You were satisfied that they were impeccable. The directors of the River Bank in St. Louis gave me a sterling report I know that they did."

"That is true," Fontaine agreed.

"Well, then, there you go," Epson said. "If the bank has found no fault with me, then this . . . this preposterous story that Mr. Ashley is spreading about me taking money from some whore, and not crediting her account, has absolutely no basis in fact."

"Whore?" Fontaine asked, screwing his face up in confusion. He looked at the letter he was holding. "And just what whore would that be, Mr. Epson?"

"The woman you said is claiming that I stole money from her. Why, she is nothing but a common whore. As a matter of fact, the house on which we held her mortgage was a house of prostitution."

"Well, now, that is interesting," Fontaine said. "For as it turns out, the money in question was supposed to be paid on a woman's house. But I made no mention of that fact. If, as you say, you have no idea what I'm talking about, how is it that you know that I was talking about a woman?"

"I . . . I just know because both she and Mr. Ashley

have tried to make trouble for me in the past," Epson stammered. "And I'm sure, should you deem it necessary to look into this most preposterous story any further, you will see that I am telling the truth."

"Yes, I'm sure that the investigation will prove you innocent," Fontaine said. "Although I must say, the amount of money Mr. Ashley claims was not credited to the woman, nine hundred fifty dollars, is remarkably close to the amount of money you deposited in your personal account when you arrived at our bank." Fontaine looked at a piece of paper. "The amount you deposited was nine hundred dollars, I believe."

"Yes," Epson said. "But of course, that was a mere coincidence. I assure you, there is nothing to this story. You will recall that when I came to work here, I told you that I had been instrumental in putting some brothel houses out of business?"

"Oh, yes, I do recall."

"I'm sure this all has to do with that. It is spite directed against me because I did my civic duty. As I say, the woman in question is a whore. You ask how I know who was behind this, even though you had not mentioned a name. I can only report that the woman in question has tried shenanigans of this sort before. It is bitterness, pure and simple."

"Well, that may be the case for the woman," Fontaine said. "But what about Mr. Ashley? I have checked on him, and I find that he is one of the most successful businessmen in St. Louis, highly respected by all in the fur-trading industry."

"Yes, but you must understand that William

Ashley cavorts, on a daily basis, with whores, trappers, hunters, wilderness guides, boatmen. And one cannot come into such constant contact with such people without being affected by them. Why, I have no doubt but that Mr. William Ashley was himself a habitué of the establishment in question."

"That is quite an accusation," Fontaine said.

"Perhaps so, but it is less damning than the false accusation he has lodged against me," Epson said.

"Why do you think someone like Ashley would make such a charge?" Fontaine asked.

"Oh, that's easy to understand. The whore, Jennie, no doubt talked him into making the accusation against me and bringing it to your attention. I'm sure that she understands that a respectable bank such as the Trust Bank of Philidelphia will have nothing to do with such a spurious accusation being lodged against a bank officer by a common whore."

"No doubt the matter will soon be cleared up," Fontaine said.

"Yes, I'm sure it will be."

"Go on back to work, Mr. Epson. I will investigate thoroughly, but quietly."

"Yes, sir, thank you," Epson said. "I shall return to work confident in my total and complete exculpation."

Shortly after he left Fontaine's office, Epson wrote a letter to a St. Louis citizen whom he knew to be of disreputable character. Such a low-class citizen, however, was exactly what he needed for the task at hand.

The letter went by stage from Philadelphia to Steubenville, Ohio, making the transit in six days. At Steubenville, the letter was put aboard a riverboat for transit to St. Louis. Traversing the Ohio and Mississippi Rivers required another fourteen days so that, twenty days after Epson mailed the letter, the St. Louis postal clerk stepped into LaBarge's saloon, carrying the letter with him.

LaBarge, who was wiping off the bar, looked up as Toomey came inside. He smiled.

"Well, well, if it isn't our illustrious mail official Mr. Toomey," LaBarge said. "This is indeed an occasion. I don't believe I've ever seen you in here before. What can I get for you, Mr. Toomey?"

"I'm not here to partake of any spirits, thank you," Toomey answered officiously. "I am here on U.S. Government business. I have come to deliver a letter."

"I've got a letter? Who from?" LaBarge asked, reaching for it.

"It isn't for you," Toomey said, pulling the letter from him.

"Well, if the letter ain't for me, what the hell are you doin' in my tavern?"

"Because I am told that the person for whom I am looking can nearly always be found here," Toomey said as he continued to look around the room. "And indeed, there he is."

When LaBarge looked in the same direction as Toomey, he blinked in surprise.

"What the hell?" he said. "Surely, you ain't talkin' about ole Ben Caviness?"

"I am," Toomey replied.

"Well, hell, that son of a bitch can't even read, can he?"

"My dear Mr. LaBarge, whether or not any of the recipients of our mail can read is of no concern of the U.S. Post Office," Toomey replied. "Our job is merely to see that the recipient receives the letter that is sent to him. Getting it read is his responsibility."

At one time, Ben Caviness considered himself a fur trapper, and he had actually spent a few winters in the mountains. But he had never been very productive in what was actually a very difficult job. Then, when his friend Percy McDill got himself killed by the one they called Preacher, Caviness gave up the trade altogether.

Now Caviness made his living by pulling odd jobs when they were available, and by resorting to petty thievery when necessary. It worked well that way because Caviness's personal needs were few. He never wasted money on clothes or personal hygiene. He lived in an empty stall at the livery, paying for it by mucking out stables. And there were a handful of houses in town where the woman of the house felt disposed toward feeding the hungry and clothing the naked, so he could show up at the back door of such a place, hat in hand, and be able to count on a meal.

With those basic needs met, any money Caviness managed to earn through the various odd jobs he performed was spent in LaBarge's Tavern. As a result, Caviness spent every available hour there, often the first to arrive when LaBarge opened his doors in the morning and the last one to leave in the evening.

Caviness was there now, at a table in the back of the room, drinking raw whiskey and talking to a few others whose own station in life was no higher. He had no idea an official of the U.S. Post Office was looking for him to deliver a letter. In fact, if questioned, Ben Caviness would have to answer truthfully that he had never received a letter in his life.

"You would be Ben Caviness?" Toomey asked, approaching the table.

"Who's askin'?" Caviness replied.

"I am an official of the U.S. Post Office," Toomey said. "And I have a letter for Mr. Ben Caviness."

Caviness looked shocked. "You have a letter for me?"

"I do indeed," Toomey replied, handing the envelope to him.

"Ha!" one of the other men at the table said. This was a man named Slater who, like Caviness, lived a hand-to-mouth existence, working as much for liquor as for food. "Who do you know that can actually write? Let alone send you a letter?"

"You'd be surprised at the high-tone people I know," Caviness replied.

Caviness opened the envelope and took out two pieces of paper. One piece of paper was obviously a letter to him, but the other looked official. He had never seen anything quite like this.

"What is this here thing?" he asked, showing it to Toomey.

Toomey looked at the paper.

"That's a bank draft for fifteen dollars."

"What does that mean? What is a bank draft?"

"That means you can take it to the bank and they will give you fifteen dollars," Toomey explained.

"The hell you say. They'll just give it to me for nothin'?"

"No, not for nothing. You will have to present them with this draft." Toomey pointed to a line on the draft. "Do you see, it is made out to you."

"I'll be damned," Caviness said, a big smile spreading across his face. "Who would give me fifteen dollars?"

"Suppose you read the letter," Toomey suggested. "I'm certain you will find the answer to your question there."

"Yeah," Caviness said. "Yeah, I'll read the letter." He began to read and, even though he was reading silently, his lips formed every word.

"What does the letter say, Caviness?" Slater asked.

Caviness looked up from the letter, then put his hand over the words.

"This here is my letter, and it ain't none of your business what it says."

# THREE

It was dark. Jennie and Dog were walking home. For many years, Jennie had made her living as a prostitute, but it wasn't a profession she chose. Born to a half-black mother in a whorehouse in New Orleans, Jennie had been sold into slavery as a very young girl.

The man who bought her, Lucas Younger, had intended to make her into a housemaid; however, as she was a very beautiful young girl, he realized early that if he played his cards right, she could be worth a lot of money to him. When she was but thirteen, he paraded her in front of a collection of the finest and wealthiest gentlemen of New Orleans. The price one man paid for the privilege of being first more than compensated Younger for her purchase in the first place.

He managed to get away with selling her for the "first" time for almost six months, until word got out as to what he was doing and he was forced to flee New Orleans, taking Jennie with him. Going by wagon from New Orleans to St. Louis, he made

Jennie available for all who would pay. In those early days, Jennie would sometimes service as many as twenty or twenty-five men in one night, all arranged by Lucas Younger.

It was during that trip north that she met Preacher for the first time. As a twelve-year-old boy, experimenting with beer for the first time, he was easy pickings for Younger, who knocked him out, put him on his wagon, and took him with him. Preacher was called Art then, and Jennie was a full year older than he was. Younger attempted to make the boy his slave, but Art got away, killing him in the escape.

A few years later, their paths crossed a second time. Jennie, now the slave of another, was still being forced to earn her keep by prostitution. At this meeting, Art managed to win Jennie in a shooting contest.

By then, Jennie knew that she was in love with him, and the thought of being his slave actually pleased her. But Art would have none of it. He gave Jennie her papers of manumission, freeing her forever. In turn, Jennie provided the boy, who was not yet known as Preacher, with his passage into manhood.

Even though Jennie was now free, she was a person with a checkered past, unable to earn a living in any way except the only way she knew. Once more she became a prostitute, but this time, working for herself, she was at least able to profit from it. Because she was frugal, she soon earned enough money to start her own brothel, which she staffed with a full complement of girls, carefully chosen for their looks and demeanor.

The House of Flowers, as she called her brothel, quickly became the most successful operation of its kind in St. Louis, and its parlors hosted some of the most influential men in the city and state. It also became a lightning rod for civic action groups, especially the Women's Auxiliary of the St. Louis Betterment League, whose president was Sybil Abernathy, wife of the president of the board of directors of the River Bank of St. Louis.

Once Jennie had her business going, she left "the line," as it was called when one was an active prostitute, doing nothing but administer her house. From that time on, the only time she was ever with a man was on those rare times when Preacher would come to St. Louis.

Jennie was in love with Preacher. She never spoke abut this to him, because she knew that it could not work out. Preacher would never be happy in a city, and she could not live in the isolation of the mountains. As a result, Preacher's visits to St. Louis were all the sweeter because they provided little windows on a life that she could only glimpse, but would never have.

When Jennie learned that Sybil Abernathy intended to force her husband to call in the loan, she took 475 dollars from her savings and presented it to the chief teller at the bank. It was enough money to pay off the mortgage on her house, thus making it fully hers, safe from the machinations of Sybil Abernathy.

What Jennie did not realize was that Preacher had also paid off her mortgage, doing so quietly because he was afraid Jennie wouldn't take the money from him. In neither case, however, was the money credited. Jennie wound up losing her house.

Now, Jennie shared a small house with her best friend, Clara. Clara, who was a few years younger than Jennie, had lived in the House of Flowers with Jennie and the other girls. Although Clara lived there, she was not, and had never been, one of the prostitutes.

By living together, the two women were not only company for each other, they also shared living expenses. Clara earned her money by working in a café, whereas Jennie earned her income by working as a seamstress. Jennie was a very good seamstress, but she had to struggle for a living. Many of the women in town, aware of her past, would have nothing to do with her.

One of the most vocal woman against her, was the one most opposed to her while she was running the whorehouse, Sybil Abernathy.

Ironically, it was Mrs. Abernathy's house Jennie was coming from tonight. Though it killed Mrs. Abernathy's soul to have to work with Jennie, the bank president's wife was in a bind. She had been invited to a party at the governor's mansion in Jefferson City, and she had nothing to wear. The only way she could get ready in time was to use Jennie's services.

She decided to do so, but insisted that Jennie

make her visits for fittings only at night. In so doing, Sybil thought it would lessen the chances that Jenny would be seen coming to or from her house.

"After all, unlike you, my dear, I do have a reputation to uphold," Mrs. Abernathy had said.

Mrs. Abernathy was a very exacting client, and if Jennie hadn't needed the money, she would have told her to get someone else to make her gown. But she did need the money, so she put up with Sybil's demands, redoing the seams, making adjustments here and changes there. It was nearly midnight by the time she left for home.

Although Mrs. Abernathy had thought she was hiring Jennie in secret, such a piece of gossip was just too juicy to keep. The news didn't come from Jennie, because she had told no one—her sense of integrity extended even to someone like Mrs. Abernathy. But others were aware of the arrangement, and soon the entire town knew that Jennie was making a special gown for Sybil Abernathy to wear to the Governor's Ball.

One of those who knew was Ben Caviness. He also knew that Mrs. Abernathy had demanded that Jennie work for her only at night. Armed with that information, Caviness waited in an alley along the route between Mrs. Abernathy's mansion and the small house that Jennie shared with Clara. As he waited, he reached down to grab hold of himself. The letter had been very specific as to what he had to do to earn the fifteen dollars the bank draft represented. It was going to be fun.

Unlike some of the larger cities back East, St. Louis had only a few street lamps, and they were in the middle of town. In the part of the city that was closest to Jennie's house, the streets were narrow and shadowed. It was particularly dark tonight, for there was no moon out. Had Dog not been with her, Jennie would have been too frightened to be out.

Dog sensed the man before he smelled him, and he smelled him before he heard anything suspicious. As they approached the alley, Dog stopped. The hackles stood up on the back of his neck. He let out a low warning growl.

"What is it, Dog?" Jennie asked. She reached down to pet him.

There was someone in the alley ahead . . . someone waiting for them. Dog didn't know who it was, but he knew that whoever it was, he was up to no good. Dog lowered his head slightly and moved ahead slowly, deliberately.

Suddenly, a man jumped out of the alley in front of them.

Jenny let out a gasp of alarm.

"Good evenin', missy," Caviness said with an evil smile.

"I know who you are," Jennie said. "You're Ben

Caviness. How dare you jump out at me! What do you mean frightening me like this?"

"Missy, you're causing a lot of trouble for a very important man, and he don't like it none," the man said.

"What are you talking about?"

"Mr. Epson don't want no more letters bein' wrote about him," Caviness said.

"I don't care what he wants. I will continue writing letters about him until I get my money back."

"Then I reckon I'm going to have to change your mind," Caviness said, taking a step toward her.

Until now, Dog had merely been watching Caviness. The moment Caviness started forward, Dog leaped toward him, snapping, and nipping him on the leg.

Startled, Caviness jumped back.

"What the hell! Call that dog off! Call him off!"

"I expect you'd better get on out of here," Jennie said.

Dog continued to growl. He wouldn't attack again unless the man attacked Jennie. But if need be, he was in position to do so. He growled and made another lunge toward the man, though he held back at the last minute.

"No! No! Call him off! Call him off!"

"Get out of here, and I'll keep him back," Jennie promised.

Caviness turned and ran, chased down the alley by Dog's barking and Jennie's laughter.

* * *

Clara was asleep when Jennie and Dog returned, but Jennie woke her up to tell what happened.

"Oh, Jennie, that is so frightening," Clara said. "You should go see Constable Billings."

"Ha," Jennie said. "A fat lot of good that will do. I have complained about that toad Epson stealing money from me, and the only thing it accomplished was to have him send Caviness after me."

"Well, to be honest about it, what can Billings do about Epson? Epson is with some bank in Philadelphia now. I'm sure that Mr. Billings has no jurisdiction over him. But he could certainly put Caviness in jail."

"For what? For wetting his pants?" Jennie asked. "Because I'm sure that's what he did when Dog got after him. Besides, if Caviness is the best Epson can come up with, then I don't think I have anything to worry about. You know what they say. Better the devil you can see than the one you can't see."

"I suppose that's true."

Jennie laughed. "And you should have seen him run! I laughed so hard that my sides hurt."

Clara laughed as well. "Oh, I wish I could've seen that," she said.

Jennie rubbed Dog behind the ears. "I'm not worried. Not as long as I have Dog to look out for me."

\* \* \*

*Philadelphia*

Once more, Theodore Epson was summoned to Joel Fontaine's office. This time, it wasn't just Fontaine, but the entire membership of the board of directors was present for the meeting. They had been talking among themselves, but they fell silent when Epson entered.

Epson looked around nervously. "You sent for me, Mr. Fontaine?"

"I did."

"To what purpose?"

"Have a seat, please," Fontaine said without directly answering Epson's concerned query.

Whereas the others were sitting in comfortable chairs around a table, the seat Fontaine offered Epson was a small, straight-backed, wooden chair, placed at some distance from the others.

"Mr. Fontaine, may I ask what is this about?" Epson asked.

"Mr. Epson, we have received another letter from Mr. Ashley of St. Louis," Fontaine said. "And this time, he included a report that Miss Jennie . . . " He looked through the letter. "There doesn't appear to be a last name."

"She has no last name," Epson said.

"No last name? Of course she has a last name. Everyone has a last name," one of the board members said.

"Many colored do not have a last name," Epson said. "She is a colored woman."

"Really? I wasn't aware of that," the board member said.

"Yes, well, let us return to business, shall we?" said Fontaine. "According to Mr. Ashley, this is a report filed by Miss Jennie, No Last Name, with a Constable Billings. Are you familiar with Constable Billings?"

"Yes, he is the chief law enforcement officer in St. Louis," Epson replied.

Fontaine cleared his throat. "Mr. Epson, this report which Miss Jennie filed with the constable alleges that you hired someone to threaten her. According to the report, he accosted her late one night. Had it not been for the fact that the lady was accompanied by a dog, he would have done her bodily harm."

"That's preposterous."

"You don't believe the lady was attacked?" Fontaine asked.

"She may well have been attacked, for St. Louis is a wild and mostly undisciplined town," Epson replied. "But I assure you, if that is the case, I had nothing to do with it. Why would I?"

"According to the report, the man who attacked her said that"—Fontaine adjusted his glasses and read directly from the letter—" 'Mr. Epson don't want no more letters wrote about him.' " Fontaine looked up. "What do you say to that?"

Epson shook his head. "I don't know what to say," he said. "Other than to say it isn't true. I have hired no one to harm her."

"Do you have any idea why she would make such a claim?"

"Yes, I have a very good idea. She is trying to extort money from me by making the claim that I took mortgage money from her without posting it to the books."

"So, it is your contention that this is part of an extortion scheme on her part?"

"Yes, her part, and William Ashley's as well. Is there any paperwork to substantiate the claim that either of them gave me any money?" Epson asked.

"Apparently not," Fontaine said. "For no such paperwork was included in the letter."

"Then I ask you gentlemen to consider this," Epson said. "We are all bankers. We deal with money every day. Our only protection against such spurious claims as these is the signed documents by which we do business. Can you imagine passing over an amount of money as large as all that without getting a signed receipt?"

There was a murmuring of agreement from the members of the board.

"Mr. Fontaine, as this is obviously an attempt at extortion, I am the aggrieved party here. I am the one who is being falsely accused. Fortunately for me, the very basis by which we do business, the signed receipt, is, by its absence in this case, proof of my innocence."

"You know, Joel, Mr. Epson has a point," one of the other board members said. "In this business we live or die by supporting documents. It seems to me contrary to everything we stand for to be accusing one of our own of a violation, when there is no evidence, such as a signed receipt to substantiate this woman's claim."

Fontaine looked at the others. "Yes, I agree. Gentlemen, I am inclined to take Mr. Epson at his word," he said. "How say you?"

Most of the board agreed, but one of the members held up his hand.

"Yes, Miller, what is it?"

"In principle, I agree. However, it just so happens that I will be making a trip to St. Louis in a few weeks. Suppose, while I am there, I visit with Mr. Ashley and this woman and talk to them in person."

"Good idea," Fontaine said. He looked up at Epson and smiled. "For now, Mr. Epson, we will take no action. I'm sure that you will be exonerated. But if Mr. Miller is going to St. Louis anyway, we may as well put this whole thing to rest once and for all. I'm sure you agree that would be the best approach."

"Yes," Epson said. Taking out his handkerchief, he dabbed at the beads of sweat along his upper lip. "Yes, I agree, that is best. And I assure you, I welcome a full inquiry into the matter."

"I was certain you would," Fontaine said. "Now, gentlemen, let us all get back to work, shall we? After all, we do have a bank to run."

That night, in his apartment, Epson walked over to the window and looked out onto the street below. What a mess he was in. He had not set out to steal anyone's money. But when the opportunity presented itself, the temptation had been just too strong to resist.

He recalled the sequence of events that had brought him to this point.

The River Bank of St. Louis had just opened for the day's business, and Epson had been at his desk for no more than five minutes when William Ashley arrived. Stepping inside the bank, Ashley looked around for a moment, then came straight over to see Epson.

"Mr. Epson, I wonder if I might have a word with you?" Ashley asked.

"Certainly, Mr. Ashley," Epson replied, standing to greet him. "It is always a pleasure to greet one of our fair city's most powerful businessmen. How are you doing, sir?"

"I'm doing fine, Epson," Ashley said.

Epson's eyes squinted, and he continued the conversation in a somewhat more guarded tone. "I must say I'm a little surprised to see you, though. I've been given to understand that you have started your own bank for the fur trappers."

Ashley shook his head in the negative. "Not at all," he said. "All I'm doing is keeping some of my trappers' earned income on the books for them."

"Isn't that what a bank does?"

"I suppose. But I'm only doing it as a favor for my trappers. Most of them don't like to carry any more money than they need."

"Nobody does," Epson said. "That's what banks are for. You could steer some of your accounts our way, you know."

"Yes, I know," Ashley replied. "And I fully intend to, over a period of time."

"Really?" Epson asked, brightening. "So, have you brought me a deposit today?"

"Not a deposit, but a payment."

"A payment? I don't understand. A payment for what? You don't have a loan here."

"It isn't for me. It is for one of your customers. It's more than a payment actually. I intend to pay off the entire mortgage."

"Why would you pay off someone else's mortgage?" Epson asked. He frowned. "Wait a minute. Have you made the loan yourself? That's it, isn't it? You're paying off the loan because you have made it yourself. You *are* going into banking."

"No. All I'm doing is paying off the loan on behalf of an interested party."

"I see. And what loan are you paying off?"

"I'm paying off the loan on the House of Flowers."

"You are paying off the whore's loan?"

"Yes."

"I don't understand. Why would you do such a thing?"

"I assure you, sir, I am not paying the loan from my own funds. As I said, I am doing so on behalf of an interested party. He doesn't want this Miss Jennie to know that he is doing it."

Epson stroked his jaw as he studied Ashley. "Are

you saying that she doesn't know her loan is being paid off?"

"That's right."

"I am curious. Who is her benefactor? Some businessman in town?"

"I don't believe I'm at liberty to say who it is," Ashley said. "I wasn't told that I couldn't tell, but I wasn't given permission to tell either. Therefore, I feel ethically bound to keep his identity a secret."

"Ha!" Epson said. "I was right, wasn't I? It is some local businessman. And of course he would make the payment through someone else if he wanted it kept secret. Like as not, it's one of the same men who, in public, call for that house to be closed, while in private, are amoung her biggest supporters. Who is it? The mayor?"

"I told you . . . I don't believe I'm at liberty to say. It doesn't matter anyway. All I intend to do is pay off the note. Now, are you going to accept the money, or what?"

"Yes, yes, of course I'll accept the money."

Later that same afternoon, Jennie herself called at the bank. Seeing her the moment she stepped through the door, Epson went over to meet her.

"Yes, Miss Jennie," he said. "Is there something I can do for you?"

"I wonder if we could speak in private for a few moments," Jennie said.

"Yes, of course we can. Come over here to my desk. We can talk there without being overheard."

There were no other women in the bank, but

there were several male customers. Most of them knew who Jennie was, and many of them had been paying customers at the House of Flowers. It would have been easy to pick out her customers, for while the others stared at Jennie in unabashed curiosity, her customers looked away pointedly, pretending they didn't even see her.

Epson led Jennie through the gate of the small, fenced-in area that surrounded his desk. He offered her a chair, then sat as well.

"Now, Miss Jennie, what is it that we can only discuss in private?"

"Recently, some people have been attempting to close down my business," Jennie said.

Epson scratched his cheek with his forefinger. "Ah, yes," he said. "You would be talking about the Women's Auxiliary of the St. Louis Betterment League."

"You know about it?"

"Yes."

"Then you also know that chief among these women is Mrs. Abernathy."

Epson nodded. "Sybil Abernathy, yes."

"Doesn't her husband have something to do with this bank?"

"Yes indeed, he is the chairman of the board of directors of the bank."

"I thought as much." Jennie opened her portmanteau and fished out a piece of paper. "According to the contract, even if I am not in arrears, the bank can call in the remainder of my loan at any time. Is that right?"

"Yes, but . . . "

"That's what I thought. That's why I want to pay off the entire loan today. That way there will be no chance for the bank to foreclose." Jennie began writing a bank draft. "I believe the amount is four hundred and seventy-five dollars."

Epson was silent for a long moment, and Jennie looked up at him questioningly. "Am I not right?" she asked.

Epson wondered what he should do. Though he had not yet posted the paperwork, he had accepted the money from William Ashley to pay off her debt. He couldn't tell her this, though, because he had been specifically instructed not to.

"Mr. Epson, is four hundred and seventy-five dollars correct?" Jennie asked again.

"Uh, yes," Epson said. He would take the money now and decide later what to do.

Jennie wrote the draft and handed it to him.

"I'll, uh, take care of this for you," Epson said.

Jennie smiled at him. "Thank you," she said. "I may be worried for no reason at all, but Mrs. Abernathy seems to be quite a determined woman. I fear she may convince her husband to exercise the foreclosure clause in the contract. I would rather just own the house free and clear, so that there is no question."

Epson nodded again. "Yes, I'm sure you are doing the right thing," he said. He picked up the draft and put it in his pocket. "I'll have the title delivered to you."

"Thank you again," Jennie said, getting up from her chair. Epson stood quickly, then walked with her to the door. He stood in the door and watched as her driver helped her climb into her carriage. Then he returned to his desk and sat there for a long moment, contemplating what he should do.

It was not until that moment that he realized what an opportunity had been dropped in his lap. He was due to leave on the very next day for his new job in Philadelphia. Neither Jennie nor, amazingly, Ashley before her had asked for a signed receipt. That meant he could leave St. Louis 950 dollars richer, and no one would ever be the wiser.

That is exactly what Epson did. And although he had come through some difficulty, it looked now as if Mr. Fontaine was willing to accept his side of the story. The only fly in the ointment was Mr. Miller's trip to St. Louis.

If Miller talked to Jennie, he might believe her version of the story. She was, after all, a very pretty young woman who could be very persuasive. If there was only some way to keep him from talking to her.

Epson stood at the window for a moment longer, and the solution came to him. It wasn't something he would have wanted to do, and it certainly wasn't anything he could do personally. But the situation had been forced upon him. Jennie herself had forced it upon him.

Turning away from the window, Epson sat at the small writing desk in his room and wrote another letter. This one was short and to the point.

*Make my problem go away.*

With the letter, he included a draft for one hundred dollars. If the intent of his message wasn't understood, the amount of money he was paying to carry out the operation would certainly make itself understood.

He just hoped that the letter reached St. Louis before Miller did.

# FOUR

A lone rider, tall and rawhide lean, sat his saddle easily as the horse picked its way down from the high country. Preacher was riding one horse and leading two more. The pack animals were carrying five hundred plews each, beaver pelts perfectly skinned, dried, and stretched so as to be of the finest quality.

The trail followed alongside a meandering brook where cool, sweet water broke white over rocks as it rushed downhill. At the end of the trail there would be Rendezvous, a gathering of mountain men and traders, trappers and fur dealers, Indians, whiskey drummers, Bible salesmen, whores, friends and strangers.

Many a mountain man spent his entire winter thinking ahead to the next Rendezvous, using it as an incentive to help him through the long period of isolation. Preacher wasn't one of them. He reveled in his isolation, and enjoyed being alone in the vastness of the Rocky Mountains. There were times, during the winter, when he would see, another trapper in the distance. Some would go out of their way to close that distance, to visit and palaver.

Preacher would not. In fact, he often changed

trails to avoid these occasional meetings. For him, Rendezvous was a necessary part of doing business. It was not two weeks of drinking, gambling, and whoring.

Those who knew Preacher best understood this about him, and accepted it. He wasn't exactly a misanthrope—he was friendly enough when he was with others, and no one could want a better friend than Preacher. He had been known to have more than a few drinks on occasion, would bet on an honest game of cards or a shooting match, and was not without experience with women. But for the most part, he was sober, upright, honest, and hardworking. These attributes were admired by all, but few could emulate them.

Preacher could smell the Rendezvous first, the aroma of coffee and cooking meat, the smell of wood and tobacco smoke, and the more unpleasant odor of scores of bodies, unwashed for months, gathered in one place.

Next, he could hear it. The sounds of people began to intrude upon the sounds of nature until soon, the babbling brook was completely overpowered by loud, boisterous talk, raucous laughter, and the high, skirling sound of a fiddle.

Finally, he rode into a clearing and saw it: men and women clad in buckskin and feathers, homespun and store-bought suits, bits of color, flashes of beads, silver and gold. Dozens of tents and temporary shelters had been erected, many of them little more than canvas flaps protruding from the wagons that had brought the traders, dealers, and goods here from back East.

In front of him, and slightly to the right, Preacher suddenly saw a flash of light and a puff of smoke At almost the same instant he heard the shot and the sound of a ball whistling past his ear.

Looking over in surprise, he saw Henri Mouchette toss his rifle aside, clawing for the pistol he had stuck down in his trousers. This was Preacher's third encounter with Mouchette this year, and it looked like this one was going to settle the score between them—one way, or the other.

Preacher leaped from his horse, not away from Mouchette, as Mouchette, might have suspected, but directly toward him. Mouchette was caught off guard by Preacher's unexpected reaction. Rather than pulling his pistol cleanly, he dropped it as he jerked it from his trousers. Preacher shoved him hard, and Mouchette staggered back, a tree breaking his fall.

Mouchette pulled his knife and held it in front of him, palm up, the knife moving back and forth slowly, like the head of a coiled snake.

"That's all right," Mouchette said. "I'd rather gut you than shoot you anyway. Shootin' kills too fast."

Preacher held a hand out in front of him, as if warding Mouchette off. He pointed at Mouchette.

"That was you that tried to shoot me a couple of months back, wasn't it?" Preacher asked.

"You're damn right it was," Mouchette answered. He nodded toward the pack horses Preacher had brought in. "By rights, them should be my plews.

You pulled my traps out of the water and set your own."

"We went through all of that," Preacher said. "My traps were there first. You pulled them out and replaced them with yours. I was only returning the favor."

"Who give you title to that creek anyway?" Mouchette asked.

"Nobody has title to any land up here," Preacher replied. "It's first come, first served, same as it's always been. And I was first there."

"You wouldn't even have know'd about it iffen you hadn't heard me talkin' about it last year."

"That's not true, and you know it. I've trapped that same creek for five winters now," Preacher said. "You can ask anyone here."

"That's right, Mouchette. I know he was there three years ago 'cause he took me in for the winter when I got stoved up," one of the trappers said. He, like several others, had been drawn in to the commotion. From other parts of the camp, people were moving as well, coming quickly to see what was going on.

"Yeah, well, it don't matter none now 'cause he ain't goin' to be trappin' it no more. I aim to split him open from his gullet to his pecker."

Mouchette lunged forward and made a swipe with his knife. The move was unexpectedly quick, and Preacher barely managed to dance back out of the way.

"Mouchette, I don't want to fight you," he said.

"If you've got a dispute with me, we can take it up with the trappers' court."

Trapper's court wasn't an official court; it was just a group of trappers who would hear arguments from both sides of a dispute, then suggest a settlement. Their suggestions had no power of law, only the power of public opinion, but for most mountain men, that was binding enough.

"Yeah, Mouchette, take it up with trappers' court," one of the others said, picking up on Preacher's suggestion.

"Nah," Mouchette replied, his evil grin spreading. "I think I'll just kill the son of a bitch, then there won't be nothing to settle." He lunged forward again, but this time Preacher was ready for him, and he easily slipped the knife thrust, then countered with a hard blow to Mouchette's ear.

Mouchette jumped back, then put his hand to his ear.

That gave Preacher the opening he needed, and he reached for his knife, only to discover that it wasn't on his belt. He looked back toward his horse and saw that his knife was in a scabbard on a belt that was hanging around the saddle pommel. His rifle was in the rifle boot, and his pistol was in the saddlebag. He was bare-handed against Mouchette.

"Well, now," Mouchette said when he noticed Preacher's predicament. "Ain't this somethin'? 'Peers to me like you've come to a knife fight without a knife."

Mouchette crouched over and held the knife in front of him, still moving it back and forth. The smile that spread across his face wasn't one of mirth, but rather one of smug satisfaction. Mouchette, who was from New Orleans, had grown up with the knife. Even in a fair fight, he might have had an advantage. But as Preacher was unarmed, there was nothing fair about this fight.

Suddenly, a knife whizzed by in front of Preacher and stuck in the tree beside him.

Preacher had no idea who it came from, and didn't know who to thank. But at this point, he had no time to consider such things. He pulled the knife from the tree, then faced Mouchette. The easy, confident smile left Mouchette's face, but the determination did not.

"Good," Mouchette said. "I like it better this way. Wouldn't be no fun in killin' you 'lessen you fight back some."

Armed, Preacher was no longer at a disadvantage. His posture mirrored that of Mouchette's. He came up on the balls of his feet, crouching slightly, holding the knife firmly—but not too tightly—palm-up in his right hand. The two men began moving around each other warily, now entirely circled by people who had come from all over the Rendezvous, drawn to the spectacle of a fight to the death.

Mouchette moved in, raised his left hand as if to shield what he was going to do, then raised his knife hand to come in behind that shield. Preacher raised his left hand to block. Seeing the smile of triumph on Mouchette's face, Preacher realized, almost too late, that he had been suckered. He had reacted exactly as Mouchette wanted him to react.

Mouchette moved his knife hand back down swiftly, as quickly as a striking snake, and he thrust toward Preacher. Preacher managed to twist away, barely avoiding the killing thrust, but not escaping entirely. He felt the knife burn as it opened a cut on his side.

Even as Preacher was avoiding Mouchette's deadly stab, he responded with a quick counterthrust. Mouchette, thinking he had won, wasn't prepared for the instantaneous response. He was wide-open to Preacher's attack. Preacher's knife went under Mouchette's ribs, slipping in cleanly, easily, all the way to the hilt. Mouchette let out a grunt, as if he'd had the breath knocked out of him. The two men stood together for a second. Then Preacher felt Mouchette falling as his body tore itself off the knife, ripping open an even larger wound.

Mouchette fell onto his side, then rolled over onto his back. He looked up at Preacher.

"I'll be damned," he said. "Boys, I come here to kill this son of a bitch. Instead, he kilt me. Now, ain't that a hell of thing?"

Mouchette wheezed a few times; then the ragged breathing stopped and his eyes, still open, glazed over.

"Whose knife?" Preacher asked, holding up the knife he had used to kill Mouchette.

When nobody spoke up, Preacher looked over toward the tree where he had gotten the knife. Grasping the point of the blade with his thumb and forefinger, he threw the knife at the tree, sticking it in the trunk in almost the same place from which he had pulled it a moment earlier.

"You done what you had to do," one of the trappers said, and several others agreed.

"Mouchette was a pain in the ass," another insisted. "If there was ever any son of a bitch needed killin', it was him."

Nodding, but with no verbal response, Preacher walked over to his horse. Taking off his shirt, he lay it across the saddle while he examined the wound on his side. Fortunately, the cut wasn't very deep, and already it had stopped bleeding. He was putting his shirt back on as someone approached him. Preacher could tell by the way he was dressed that this was one of the traders from back East.

The trader looked over the pack animals. "Looks like you had a good season," he said.

"Tolerable," Preacher replied.

The trader looked at the pelts more closely, folding them back to examine several of them.

"More than tolerable, I'd say. These are some of the best I've seen brought in since I been here."

"Thanks."

"You the one they call Preacher?" the man asked.

"I am," Preacher said.

"I work for Mr. Ashley. William Ashley? I believe you know him."

"Yes, I know him," Preacher said.

Preacher had done business with Ashley many times before. In fact, he had once negotiated a peace with the Indians for Ashley and his traders.

In this world of few contacts, and even fewer friends, William Ashley was a man that Preacher would count as a friend.

"Mr. Ashley said to treat you fair."

"He always has. That's his way," Preacher replied.

"Oh, and I almost forgot. He told me to give this to you," the trader added, handing an envelope to Preacher.

"Thanks," Preacher said.

"Hey, Preacher," one of the others called. "We got us a shootin' match comin' up tonight. Ever'one puts in a dollar, winner take all. What do you say?"

"What are you invitin' him for, Drew?" one of the others said. "You know he always wins."

"I know," Drew said. "But they's always them that'll bet he won't win, so what I lose by not winnin' myself, I make up by bettin' on a sure thing."

"Yeah, I never thought of that. What about it, Preacher? You aim to get in on the shootin'?"

"I reckon not," Preacher responded. He put some moss onto the cut, then put on a fresh shirt. "But thanks for the invite."

As the trader continued to look through the pelts, Preacher sat on a fallen log. Setting the envelope down, he took out his pipe, poured in some tobacco, tamped it down, lit it, and took a few puffs before he turned his attention back to the letter. Finally, he reached for it, opened the envelope, pulled out the letter, and began to read.

*Dear Preacher,*
   *It is with great sadness that I must inform*
*you of the death of our mutual friend, Jennie.*

"Oh, shit," Preacher said, pinching the bridge of his nose.

"Somethin' wrong?" the trader asked.

"You don't know what's in this letter?" Preacher asked, holding it up.

The trader shook his head. "Wasn't my letter, wasn't my place to read it," he said.

"How long ago was it written?"

"I'm not sure. Six weeks, two months maybe. I've had it at least six weeks."

Six weeks, Preacher thought. Jennie had been dead for at least six weeks, and he didn't even know it. Several times, something would happen that would remind him of her, and he would hear her laugh, or see her smile—if only in his memory. But the ability to enjoy his thoughts and remembrances of her only worked if she was alive.

"Say, Preacher, do you mind if I take these pelts on over to my wagon so I can count and grade them?"

"What? No, no, go ahead, I don't mind," Preacher replied distractedly. Reluctantly, he returned to the letter.

*I wish I could tell you that Jennie died peacefully, but I cannot. She was murdered, Preacher, in a way so vile as to defy any attempt to describe by written words. There were two of them, but one of them got away.*

*I'm sure you remember Ben Caviness, for you had such a difficult time with him when he was part of your trapping party. Nobody knows for sure who the one is that got away, but I believe it was Ben Caviness.*

*The problem is, what with Jennie being a whore and all, I'm afraid there will be no justice.*

*Preacher, I know what store you set by Miss Jennie, and I'm sorry to have to be the one to tell you such sad news, but I knew you would want to know.*

*Your friend,*
*William Ashley*

Folding the letter, Preacher got up and walked over to stick it down into his saddlebag. He glanced over toward where the fight had taken place, and saw that a couple of men were already digging a grave for Mouchette.

How odd, this sensation. Moments earlier, he had been locked in a life-and-death struggle, a struggle that he barely survived. Yet now, it seemed so remote to him that it could have happened to someone else. His thoughts were only of Jennie.

He wondered where Jennie was buried, and if anyone had shown up to say a few words over her. He hoped that they had, but he knew that it would take a brave preacher to risk the ire of his parishioners in order to pray over one of St. Louis's most notorious women.

Preacher felt an overwhelming sense of sorrow

over her loss. Then, as he considered the fact that she'd been was murdered, the sorrow gave way to anger.

He walked over to the trader's wagon, where the trader was busy counting out and sorting Preacher's pelts.

"It's amazing," the trader said. "All of your pelts are of the very highest quality."

"How quickly can you pay me for them?" Preacher asked.

"Well, if you will take a marker against Ashley, I can pay you right away."

"I'll take his marker," Preacher said.

"Very well, I'll make one out for you."

"Before you left St. Louis, did you hear about Jennie getting killed?"

"Oh, heavens, yes," the trader replied. "It was all anyone talked about for a while. It's a shame about her. Such a pretty young girl."

"Yeah, a shame," Preacher said.

He thought about what Ashley said in his letter about Jennie not getting justice. William Ashley was wrong. There would be justice, all right. It would be Preacher's Justice.

# FIVE

*Ste. Genevieve, Missouri*

The doctor in Ste. Genevieve daubed more wagon grease onto what was left of Ben Caviness's ear.

"It's a good thing you came to me when you did," the doctor said. "This ear was near to mortifying."

"Yeah, well, it's been hurtin' somethin' awful."

"What did you say caused this again?"

"A bear," Caviness said. "I run up against a bear and he mauled me."

"Looks more like something bit this ear off, rather than clawing it off," the doctor said.

"Yeah, that's what I mean. The bear bit it off."

"You're lucky he didn't bite off your whole head."

"Do you have to talk so much, Doc? Just patch up the ear and stop the talkin'."

"I was just being friendly," the doctor said. "It's always good to be friendly with your patients. Puts them in a good frame of mind."

"Yeah, well, it don't work with me."

"I can see that it doesn't," the doctor said. He

straightened up, then looked at Caviness. "That'll be one dollar," he said.

"One dollar!" Caviness exploded. "One dollar for a handful of grease you could get offen any wagon wheel?"

"It's not the grease you're paying for. It's the knowing what to do with the grease," the doctor said.

"Yeah, yeah," Caviness said. Still grumbling, he paid the doctor the dollar, then left the doctor's house and walked down to the river's edge to wait for the next boat to come through.

When Caviness got the second letter from Epson, the one that said, "Make my problem go away," he knew what Epson was asking for. Epson was paying him one hundred dollars to kill Jennie.

One hundred dollars seemed like an enormous amount of money then, because it seemed like a simple job. After all, how hard could it be to kill a woman?

Caviness knew about the dog. He had encountered the dog before. But he figured that he and Slater should be able to handle the dog with little difficulty. After all, the dog hadn't actually attacked him the last time. The dog had merely barked and growled.

That sure wasn't the case this time. The dog had attacked immediately. But even as Caviness was stabbing the dog, slashing away at him, the dog was ripping out Slater's throat. Slater was killed before he could say a word.

What started out to be an easy job turned into a nightmare. Slater was dead, and Caviness had to face the dog alone. The dog turned on Caviness, and Caviness threw up an arm to guard his neck. He felt an intense pain in his left ear; then he managed to shoot the dog. The dog fell to the ground—whether dead or alive, Caviness didn't know. All he knew was that the dog was away from him.

Caviness had planned to have a little fun with Jennie, but it was too late for that now. Dog had seen to that. Caviness was bleeding so badly that he was in danger of passing out from blood loss. When he finally did turn his attention to the whore, the expression on her face reflected the horror of the moment.

Caviness was a terrible sight to behold. He had blood all over his face, arms, and hands. The side of his head was covered with blood too, as well as an ugly little piece of shredded flesh that was the only indication of what had once been an ear.

Caviness made one mighty sweep with his knife, not only cutting her jugular, but nearly decapitating her. Leaving Dog dying, and Jennie and Slater dead, Caviness left the scene of the crime. Stealing a rowboat, Caviness started downriver. He had no immediate plan in mind. At this point, all he wanted to do was get out of St. Louis.

He wasn't sure when he came up with the plan of going to Philadelphia to see Mr. Theodore Epson. But the more he thought of it, the better the idea became. He would get more money from Epson. He figured losing an ear should be worth a lot of money. And if Epson thought otherwise, then all

Caviness would have to do is go to the law with the letter Epson had sent him.

Caviness wasn't even sure where Philadelphia was, though he had a vague suspicion that one could get there, or nearly so, merely by taking a riverboat. It was his intention to take the next one that stopped in Ste. Genevieve. When he heard the whistle of the approaching boat, Caviness put his hand over the bandaged ear and walked down to wait for it. There was no one ashore selling tickets, but the moment he stepped on board, the purser arranged his passage for him. He found out from the purser that the boat couldn't take him all the way to Philadelphia as he had hoped, but he would take it as far as he could.

Once they were under way, Caviness walked to the bow of the boat and watched the river roll underneath them. He had never been to Philadelphia. He had never been to any city any larger than St. Louis. He wondered if they had whorehouses in Philadelphia.

*Kansas City*

Jeb Law had his back to the bar as he was putting bottles of whiskey in their place.

"What do you have that isn't poison?" someone asked from behind him.

Jeb didn't turn around.

"Ain't you ever heard the temperance lectures,

mister? It's all poison, some of it is just quicker than the other," Jeb replied.

"Well, if you got anything that won't eat through the glass before I can get it down, I'll have a drink."

This time Jeb recognized the voice, and he turned around, then smiled broadly as he stuck his hand across the bar. "Art!" he said. "Well, if you ain't a sight for tired ole eyes."

"Hello, Jeb," Preacher said, shaking Jeb's hand. "How are things here in Westport?"

"It's Kansas City now," Jeb corrected, reaching under the bar to pull out a special bottle to pour Preacher's drink. "Nobody calls it Westport anymore. Come to think of it, nobody calls you Art anymore either, do they? It's Preacher, isn't it?"

"That's the handle folks seem to have hung on me," Preacher said, reaching for some money.

Jeb held out his hand, palm facing Preacher. "Your money ain't no good with me, Preacher," he said. "This drink is on the house."

"I'll let you buy me the first one," Preacher said. "Then I'll buy us both one."

Jeb smiled. "Sounds good enough to me," he said. "What brings you to Kansas City? You don't come this far east all that often. From what I hear, you're about as fixed in those mountains as one of them aspen trees."

"I'm on my way to St. Louis," Preacher said. "Thought I might find a place to board my string here, then take a boat."

"What have you got?"

"Good riding horse, two good pack animals."

"How long you plannin' on being gone?"

Preacher shook his head. "Well, that's just it. I don't know as I can answer that question."

Jeb smiled. "That ain't like you not to have a clear plan of what you're goin' to do," he said.

"Oh, I've got me a clear plan of what I'm goin' to do, all right," Preacher said. "I just don't know how long it's going to take me to do it."

Preacher killed the rest of his drink, and Jeb set another glass on the table, filled both of them, then put his special bottle back under the bar.

"Sounds a little mysterious," Jeb said. He took the coin Preacher gave him, then picked up his glass and held it out toward Preacher. "Here's to you, my friend," he said.

Preacher nodded and touched his glass to Jeb's. "And to old times," he replied.

Jeb tossed the drink down, then wiped the back of his hand across his mouth.

"Now, what is it you're a'plannin' on doin', if you don't mind my askin'?"

"I reckon you heard about what happened to Jennie," Preacher replied.

"Jennie?" For a second Jeb squinted, then his face registered recognition. "You're talking about that pretty little gal used to run the House of Flowers back in St. Louis?"

"Yes."

"No, don't know as I've heard anything about her lately."

"She's dead, Jeb," Preacher said.

"Dead? Oh, the hell you say," Jeb replied. He

shook his head. "That's a damn shame. She was a fine woman, for all that she was a whore. Wait a minute. You set some store by her, didn't you?"

"Yeah, I did. I set quite a store by her," Preacher said.

"I'm real sorry to hear about her dyin'," Jeb said. "She come down with somethin', did she?"

"She was murdered."

"Murdered," Jeb repeated. Without being told, he reached under the bar, pulled out the bottle, and refilled their glasses one more time. "Does anyone know who done it?"

"I got a letter from Mr. Ashley," Preacher said. "He thinks Caviness may have had something to do with it."

"Caviness? Ben Caviness?"

"Yes."

"Well, from what I remember about the son of a bitch, he's mean enough to do something like that. Come to think of it, didn't he trail with you one season?"

"Yes, he and his partner Percy McDill."

"McDill, yeah, I remember him. Hell, he was as ornery as Caviness from what I can recall. Whatever happened to him?"

"I killed him," Preacher said. "I just wish I had killed Caviness the same time."

"What happened?"

Preacher took another drink, then stared off, as if looking into the distance. "The son of a bitch tried to rape Jennie."

"Yeah? Then the son of a bitch needed killin'. I'd like to hear about it, if you don't mind the tellin'."

"No, I don't mind the tellin'," Preacher said as he started the story.

*Two years earlier, at Rendezvous*

In the darkness, illuminated only by a single candle, Jennie faced a terrifying apparition. Percy McDill burst into her tent and now moved toward her, his face twisted by lust and anger into a grotesque mask. The candle's reflection in his dark eyes gave Jennie the illusion of staring into the very fires of hell. She stepped backward, but found little room to maneuver in the confines of the tent.

Jennie screamed.

Outside, Preacher heard a woman's scream. It came from a nearby tent. It startled him—not because of the cry itself, but because he thought he recognized the voice of the woman who screamed. But it couldn't be. It couldn't be who he thought it was. Could it?

Running in the direction of the noise, Preacher wondered what Jennie would be doing out here. He was certain she was in St. Louis, and yet, something about the scream touched his very soul. He hurried toward the tent.

***

McDill lunged, clamping his dirty hand over her mouth. Jennie bit his hand and he ripped it away, howling like a wounded animal. She screamed again. Outside the tent she could hear people moving around, and she hoped someone would come to help her. She fought back, pummeling his chest and face with her hands, but he was so big and strong that it had no effect.

"You bitch!" he sneered, cradling his wounded hand. "I was gonna pay you, whore that you are, but now I'm not—I'm gonna take it for free."

"Stay away," she warned. "For your own good, mister. I don't want to hurt you."

"Ha! You don't want to hurt me?" he said with a lopsided, drunken grin. "Tell me, bitch, how are plannin' on hurtin' me?"

She couldn't stand the smell of him, and his ugly leer. Yet she realized that she had to be careful, that she couldn't rile him even more—or else he was liable to kill her. She had known men like him for her entire life.

She gathered what composure she could, and brushed a fall of hair back from her face. She forced herself to smile at him.

"Look, you're right, whoring is my business. But I was just getting ready for bed and I must look a mess. Why don't you go away now, give me a chance to get ready, then you can come back later," she said.

"No way, little lady. I'm here and here I stay. You'll get to like me when you know me better. I promise."

Jennie doubted that she would ever be able to

bear the sight of this man, let alone like him. He was grotesque, and it didn't matter that he was drunk. She had met this kind before, and he reminded her of her old master, among others.

"But you'll like me better if you give me a chance to get ready for you," Jennie said, making one last attempt to get through to him.

"I like you fine just the way you are," he said, starting toward her again.

Jennie felt the world closing in on her and smelled blood in the air; she could only hope it wasn't her own. Again she screamed for help.

At that moment the tent flaps opened, and it was as if God himself had heard her plea. The one man in the world whom she truly loved stepped inside. It was Preacher, the man she had known as a boy— the man who was a part of her life even when they were not together.

McDill turned to see the man he hated most in the world—the man he had thought was dead— moving at him swiftly and angrily. He ducked to avoid Preacher's first swing, and came up with a hard punch of his own, taking Art off guard, smashing into his chin. He laughed as the younger man staggered backward.

"Well, now, if it ain't my ole pal," McDill said. "Are you goin' to preach to me, Preacher? Are you going to save my soul?" He laughed.

Preacher got to one knee and shook his head, trying to clear away the cobwebs of the hammerlike blow. He stared up at McDill, and at the hideous leering grin on his face.

McDill held his hand out and curled his fingers, tauntingly inviting Preacher toward him.

"Well, come on, Preacher," he said. "Come on, you son of a bitch. I'm going to beat you to a pulp."

His head cleared, Preacher leaped up again and charged at McDill. He buried his head in McDill's midsection and both men went crashing to the ground.

Preacher scrambled to his feet and grabbed McDill by the collar, then dragged him outside. He wanted to take this confrontation away from Jennie. By now a crowd, drawn by the screams and the commotion, had gathered just outside. They surrounded the two men, who were locked in a deadly confrontation.

The crowd cheered for Preacher and jeered McDill. McDill managed to get to his feet, and the big man charged like a bull. Preacher stepped out of the way, and McDill went hurtling into the crowd.

Laughing at his awkwardness, the men in the crowd caught McDill and pushed him back into the circle of combat. The two men faced each other again, and Preacher punched him as hard as he could. McDill doubled over. Preacher landed a strong right to McDill's jaw, straightening him out and sending him back on his heels, massaging the hand that had struck the blow.

Ben Caviness was watching with the others in the crowd. He wanted to go to the aid of his friend, but he dared not, for fear of the retribution of others. McDill was on his own now. Caviness melted away into the growing darkness. Even as the fight was going on behind him, he saddled his horse. If Preacher won, he might come after Caviness. If McDill won, he would want to know why Caviness didn't help him. Under the circumstances, Caviness knew that this was no place for him to be.

Jennie came out of her tent then. Preacher turned toward her, then held his hand out, as if telling her to stay away. "Jennie, stay back, keep out of the way!" he cautioned.

Preacher looked away from McDill for just that quick second. McDill pulled his long-bladed hunting knife from its sheath and lunged at Preacher, the knife pointing at his guts. Now, enraged and humiliated by the beating he was taking from this younger and smaller man, McDill was more animal than human.

Jennie saw McDill and called out to Preacher: "Look out! He has a knife!"

Preacher turned just in time to see the blade flash in the flickering light of the nearby fires. He reared back to avoid the killing knife, then circled his enemy bare-handed. Someone from the crowd tossed him a stick. Preacher used it as a defensive weapon, swinging it at McDill to keep him at bay. With one swing, McDill's knife chopped the stick in half.

"What are you goin' to do now, Preacher?" McDill taunted, holding the knife out in front of him. He moved the point back and forth slightly, like the head of a coiled snake. "You think that little stick is going to stop me? I'll whittle it down to a toothpick, then I'll carve you up."

Preacher realized then that he had no choice, he must fight this madman on his terms—no rules, any weapon at hand, and to the death. He drew his own knife and held it up, showing it to Percy McDill. He said, without words, that he intended to kill the man who had threatened Jennie.

Suddenly, it seemed as if McDill had sobered up. The taunting, leering grin left his face and he became deadly serious and focused. With a steady hand, he held his own knife up, challenging his opponent. His face was now a mask of calm determination.

"You'd better start preachin' your own funeral, Preacher," McDill said. "It's time for you to die."

Now, for the first time, Preacher grinned. It was neither taunting nor leering. Instead, it was confident, and it completely unnerved McDill. "I don't think so, McDill," Preacher said easily. "I think you are the one who is going to die."

"I'm going to kill you, and that damned mutt of yours," McDill said with false bravado, trying now to bolster his own courage.

Out of the corner of his eye, Preacher could see Dog, standing on the edge of the watching crowd. The young mountain man put aside all thoughts other than one: McDill must die. Trying to hurt Jennie was the last evil thing this son of a bitch would ever do.

The two men circled each other like gladiators in a Roman arena. The crowd became silent. Even Jennie, who watched in horror, could neither speak nor cry out. Dog stood at alert. He could have attacked

McDill, but somehow seemed to sense that this was something Preacher needed to do by himself.

McDill moved first. He swung his blade at Preacher, missing his face by only a few inches. Preacher felt the wind of the swift knife blade and jerked his head back. In almost the same movement, he swung his own knife low and hard, aiming for McDill's belly. He missed.

The big man then punched Art on the side of his head.

Art was stunned, and for a second he couldn't see anything. He backed away quickly to avoid the oncoming McDill, then stepped to one side. As McDill shot past him, he stabbed with his knife blade and felt it slip into McDill's midsection.

He pushed the knife in as far as it could go, then held it there. The two men stood together, absolutely motionless, for a long moment. Preacher felt McDill's warm blood spilling over his knife and onto his hand.

Howling like a stuck pig, McDill pulled himself off the knife. He stepped back several feet, then came back toward Preacher. But before he could even lift his own knife, he gasped, dropped the knife, and put his hand to his wound. Blood filled his cupped palms, then began oozing from his mouth as well. His eyes turned up in their sockets, showing the bloodshot whites.

From her position by the front of her tent, Jennie looked at McDill's eyes. They had caught the reflection of the campfires, and once more, she had the illusion of staring into the pit of hell. She shuddered, wrapping her arms around herself as she realized that, within minutes, McDill would be in hell.

"Damn . . . you . . . " McDill managed to gurgle through the blood and spit that filled his mouth. "Damn . . . "

Preacher took one step toward the dying man, then stopped. McDill's big body shuddered, then collapsed in a heap on the ground. Beneath him, the blood pooled darkly from his leaking wound.

Jennie ran up and threw her arms around Preacher, kissing him. He stood still, unable to take his eyes off the crumpled heap that had once been a man.

Finally, he spoke. "Where did Caviness go?"

"I think we will never see him again," said one of the men in the crowd. "I saw him sneak away like a dog."


"That's one hell of a story," Jeb said when Preacher finished with the telling. "You're plannin' on goin' after Caviness, you say?"

"Yes," Preacher said.

"What are you going to do with your string?"

"I don't know, sell them, board them. I was hoping you would have an idea."

"I'll keep your animals for you," Jeb said. "If you don't come back by next season, I'll sell 'em and hold the money for you, after takin' out what it took me to feed 'em."

"I appreciate that," Preacher said.

"Now, what do you say to me'n you go down to the Blue Hole Café and havin' us some supper?" Jeb offered.

Preacher smiled. "Sounds good to me."

# SIX

The enticing aroma of pork cooking over a hickory fire drifted down the street to them even before they reached the café known as Blue Hole. Blue Hole was a wood-frame building with a shake roof and a wide-plank floor. The cooking pit was just behind the building, and the aromatic smoke the cooking produced was the best advertisement the café had.

A large woman, known as Aunt Molly, greeted the two men when they came into the cafe. "Howdy, Jeb," she said, smiling at the saloon keeper.

There was only one empty table, and it was covered with leftover bones, but Aunt Molly led them to it, scooped up the bones, then used a soiled cloth to wipe the table.

"Who's your young, good-lookin' friend?" she asked, smiling over at Preacher.

"This here is Preacher," Jeb said.

Aunt Molly looked at Preacher with interest. "Preacher? Are you a man of the cloth?"

"No, ma'am," Preacher replied.

"Oh, heavens!" Aunt Molly said with an expression that was almost awe. "Are you that mountain man folks call Preacher?"

"That's who he is, all right," Jeb said.

"You're getting' yourself quite a reputation," Aunt Molly said. "They say you're the ridin'st, shootin'st, fightin'st, trappin'st, dancin'st, handsomest man in all the mountains." She switched the handful of gnawed bones from her right hand to her left, then reached out with a greasy palm. "I don't know about all the rest, but I'll vouch for the handsome part," she said. "I'm right pleased to meet you, Preacher."

Preacher hesitated but a moment before he took her hand. Her effusive description of him was a little embarrassing, but he knew that she meant well. He extended his hand to hers. "I'm very pleased to meet you," he said.

At the next table, two men got up to leave.

"You gents come back now, you hear?" Aunt Molly called to them.

One of them grunted in reply.

"What have you got that's good, Aunt Molly?" Jeb asked.

"We got some ribs just ready to come off," Aunt Molly replied. "Perhaps you're a'smellin' 'em now?"

Jeb smiled. "The whole town is smellin' them."

"Well, I certainly hope so," Aunt Molly replied with a little laugh.

"Tell you what. How 'bout you bring us a side of ribs, some beans, bread, and coffee?" Jeb ordered.

"Help yourself to the coffee, and I'll go back to get the ribs," Aunt Molly said.

As Aunt Molly headed out back, Jeb walked over to the coffeepot, where he poured two cups. He returned to the table, a steaming mug in either hand.

***

Three men were having a conversation at a hitching rail just up the street from the Blue Hole. One was tall, with a very dark, scraggly beard. The other two were somewhat shorter and clean-shaven. They were the two who had just left the Blue Hole.

"You sure it's Preacher?" the tall, scraggly-bearded man asked.

"Oh, yeah, it's him all right," one of the other two said. "I mind seein' him at a Rendezvous a year or so back."

"Sides which, Jeb's the one pointed him out. They say Jeb's known him for a long time," the other man said.

The tall man stroked his beard and smiled. "Well, now," he said. "Looks like I just got me a streak o' luck, don't it?" He took out his pistol and began loading and charging it.

"Luke, I sure hope you know what you're doin', goin' after Preacher like this. I've heard of him. They say he's one slippery fella to try 'n get ahold of. Lots of men have tried it, and lots of men have died."

"I ain't plannin' on dancin' with the son of a bitch, so I won't be tryin' to get ahold of him. I plan on just puttin' a ball in his brain," Luke said as he continued to prepare his pistol. "Now, are you men with me, or not?"

"I ain't got no quarrel with 'im," one of the others said.

"I didn't have no quarrel with Roland Peters

either," Luke replied. "But when you went up against him last year, I was with you."

"Luke's right, George. He was right there with us."

"Roland Peters wasn't no Preacher," George replied.

"If they's three of us go after the son of a bitch, they's no way he can handle us all. Hell, he's only got one charge in his pistol."

George sighed. "All right, I'll back you. But you're the one that's goin' to call him out."

"Don't worry, I'll do that, all right," Luke replied.

Back in the Blue Hole Café, Preacher, unaware of the three who were plotting against him, continued his conversation with Jeb.

"You know anything else about Miss Jennie getting murdered?" Jeb asked as they waited for their dinner to be served. Preacher had chosen the chair that faced the front of the café, which meant that Jeb had his back to the door. "I mean, did the letter tell you how it happened, why it happened? Anything like that?"

"This is all I know," Preacher said, taking Ashley's letter from a pocket and handing it across the table to him.

Jeb took out a pair of spectacles, fitted them carefully over one ear at a time, then read the letter. He concentrated on it for a moment, then clucked sympathetically. "I'm real sorry to hear about that," he said, handing the letter back. "I didn't really know her all that well. Did Miss Jennie have any family as you know about?"

Preacher shook his head. "Nobody that I know about," he said. "I reckon me'n her friend Clara's about the only ones that she was really close to."

"You!" a loud, angry voice suddenly shouted, disturbing the peace of the café.

Looking toward the front door, the patrons of the café saw that a tall man with a black, scraggly beard had just stepped through the front door of the café.

"Are you the one they call Preacher?"

The man was holding his hand down by his side, but Preacher saw at once that there was a pistol in his hand. And even from where he sat, he could see that the pistol was cocked. He could only assume that it was also primed.

"I'm the one they call Preacher," he said.

"My name is Luke Mouchette. That name mean anything to you?"

Jeb, who was sitting with his back to the door, turned to look.

"Jeb, I reckon you better move away," Preacher said quietly.

Instead of moving out of the way, Jeb turned toward the intruder. "Look here, Mr Mouchette, I don't know what this is about but . . . "

"Jeb, get the hell out of the way! Now!" Preacher insisted, interrupting Jeb in mid-sentence.

Jeb got up from the table and walked over to the side of the room. He wasn't the only one to move, as every other table in the café emptied. The patrons, left their food on the tables, as they scrambled to get out of the way.

"You didn't answer me, Preacher," Mouchette said. "Have you ever heard my name before?"

"Yes, I've heard it," Preacher said, easily.

"Where have you heard it?"

"I killed a low-assed, mealy-mouthed, piss-complexioned, maggot-infested son of a bitch by the name of Mouchette," Preacher said, his voice clipped and cold. "I take it there is some connection?"

"He was my brother," Mouchette said. "He was my brother, and you kilt him, you son of a bitch!"

"He needed killing," Preacher said.

"Yeah, well, so do you," Mouchette shouted. He raised his pistol and aimed it at Preacher, who had so far, made no effort to move.

Suddenly there was a loud bang . . . not from Mouchette's gun, but from under the table. A hole appeared in the table and chips of wood flew as a ball passed through the tabletop. That same ball plunged into Mouchette's chest and he staggered back toward the door, a surprised look on his face, blood pumping from the wound. In a reflexive action, Mouchette fired his pistol as he staggered back, sending the ball into the wide-planked floor.

From just outside the café, George saw Luke stagger back. With his own pistol drawn, he started toward the front door.

\*\*\*

There was a large hole in the top of the table where Preacher had been sitting. Preacher stood then, and as he did so, everyone could see that he was holding a smoking pistol in his hand.

"How the hell did you do that?" Jeb asked, pointing to the pistol.

Preacher didn't respond to Jeb's question. Instead, moving quickly, he hurried to the front door and stood to one side of it. A man came running in.

"You son of a bitch!" George shouted, pointing his gun toward the table where Preacher had been sitting. Not seeing him there, George raised his pistol in confusion. He had only a second to be confused, though, because Preacher hit him right between the eyes with the butt of his own pistol.

George fell back upon the body of Luke Mouchette, and as he fell, Preacher dropped his own gun and grabbed George's.

Rearmed, Preacher stepped out the front door, where a third man fired at him. The bullet whizzed passed Preacher's head and buried itself in the door frame right beside Preacher's head. Preacher fired back and the man went down.

With no other adversaries on the scene, Preacher stepped back inside, still holding the smoking gun. He tossed it to one side, picked up his own spent weapon, and walked back over to the table, cognizant now of everyone staring at him in shock and awe.

Aunt Molly was standing by the table holding a plate of ribs, her eyes wide, a shocked expression on her face. Smoke from the discharges gathered in a billowing cloud under the ceiling.

Quickly and carefully, Preacher reloaded his pistol. From outside, voices could be heard as people started running toward the café. When the first man came in, he stepped back in fear and surprise when he saw that Preacher had leveled his gun toward him.

"Hold on! Hold on!" the man shouted, putting his hands up in the air. "I mean you no harm."

Slowly, Preacher lowered his pistol, then nodded for the man to come on inside.

Luke Mouchette was on the front porch, his head hanging down over the step, his feet just inside the door. The right foot was pointing straight up, the left foot cocked to one side. There was a hole worn in the sole of his left boot. The man Preacher had knocked out was just now coming to, and he stood up, shook his head a few times, then walked away, leaving the café behind him. He didn't even look down at the body of the second man Preacher had shot.

Another man hurried over to the café. Stopping on the front porch, he looked down at Luke's body, then came on inside. He was wearing a badge.

"What happened here?" he asked.

"This here fella didn't have no choice, Sheriff," one of the café patrons said quickly. "Them three others all come for him."

"That's the truth of it, Paul," Jeb said. "We was all witnesses."

The sheriff stood there for a moment, then looked at Preacher. "Do you know why he come for you?"

"I killed that one's brother," Preacher replied, pointing to Luke.

"Where'd you do that?"

"At Rendezvous, out in the Rockies."

"At Rendezvous, you say?"

Preacher nodded.

"Trappers is normally pretty straight about things. If you killed him at Rendezvous and they let you go, you was probably in the right," the sheriff said. "Besides which, ain't no concern of mine what happened out there. And if all these folks say you was in the right here, I don't plan to do nothin' about this either."

"Thanks," Preacher said.

"I'd appreciate it, though, if you'd put the gun away."

Preacher stared at his pistol for a moment, then stuck it back in his belt.

The sheriff looked at Aunt Molly. "I'll get the undertaker down here to pull the body off your front porch," he said.

Aunt Molly chuckled. "No hurry," she said. "Long as he's out there, folks will come have a look. And when they do, why, they'll just naturally want to come in and have dinner."

The others laughed.

"Lord, I hope not, Aunt Molly," the sheriff said. "Else you'll be draggin' anyone that gets shot down here."

More laughter as the sheriff left the café.

"I'm sorry about the table," Preacher said to Aunt Molly after the sheriff was gone. "If you tell me how much it is, I'll pay to have another one built for you."

"I reckon a dollar will pay for your food and fix the table," Aunt Polly said.

Preacher pulled out a silver dollar and handed it to her, then reached for the plate of ribs.

"Thanks," he said. "This looks good."

# SEVEN

*On board the riverboat* Nathanial Pyron

At first, Caviness thought that the interest people were paying him was because of morbid curiosity over the fact that he was obviously missing an ear. But the second day into the trip, he was standing at the railing when the captain and two deckhands approached him.

"Mister, you want to tell us how you lost that ear?" the boat captain asked.

Caviness put his hand to the wound on the side of his face.

"What business is it of yours how I lost it?" he asked.

"Well, you see, the thing is, some of our passengers are down from St. Louis. And according to them, there was a young woman murdered up there recently. But it turns out, she had a dog who defended her. The dog bit the ear off her attacker."

"Yeah, well, I don't know nothin' about that," Caviness said. "I got this ear bit off by a bear."

"That may be," the captain said. "But I intend to put you in irons now until we get to Cape Girardeau.

There, I'll turn you over to the constable, and he can take you back up to St. Louis until you get all this worked out."

As the men started toward him, Caviness hesitated only for a moment. Then he climbed onto the rail and leaped down into the Mississippi River.

"The son of a bitch is getting away!" one of the deckhands shouted, and he and the other two ran to the railing. Looking down into the river, they could see only the roiling water, but no sign of the man without an ear.

"Where is he? Where did he go?"

"I think we can forget about him, boys," the captain said. "The currents and eddies are so strong right through here that it's damn near impossible to swim. More'n likely he's drowned already."

"Yeah, well, that's good enough for him," the first deckhand said.

"If he's the one that done the killin'," the second said.

"He's the guilty one, all right," the captain said. "Otherwise, he wouldn't of jumped over like that.

*On the Missouri River, on board the* Missouri Belle

Preacher booked passage from Kansas City to St. Louis on the steamboat *Missouri Belle*. He had enough money to afford first-class passage, and could have easily occupied the most luxurious stateroom. The fact that he chose not to was due less to parsimony than to the fact that he was genuinely more comfortable on the open deck than in one of the fancy staterooms.

While in Kansas City, Preacher got himself some new clothes, though his new duds, like those that he'd gotten rid of, were made of buckskin. He rented a bathtub and got himself cleaned up, even going to the barber for a haircut and a shave. As a result, he cut quite a handsome figure when he stepped aboard the *Missouri Belle.* Two of the passengers, Misses Emma Purdy and Cynthia Cain, took note of him, smiling at him from behind the fans they were carryng.

The two very pretty young ladies were from well-to-do families in Kansas City. Their families, believing that Kansas City was too provincial a town for them, were sending them to St. Louis for finishing school.

Although the young women had noticed Preacher the moment he came on board, they made no effort to approach him, believing that he, as most other men they had encountered, would make the first move. When, by the evening of the second day, it became obvious to them that he wasn't going to come to them, they approached him.

Preacher was standing by the rail, looking at the shoreline. Preacher had been through this country many times before, and was sorry to see that even here, civilization was beginning to creep in. Now he saw farmhouses and cultivated land where, on previous voyages up and down the river, there had been nothing but wilderness. He wondered how long it would be before civilization, and all its ills, encroached upon the West that he knew.

Though the scene was bucolic, it wasn't silent. The boat was a cacophony of sound as it moved down river. The steam-relief valve was booming, the engine clattering, and the side-mounted paddle wheels were slapping against the water. Because of all the noise, he didn't hear the two women approach. The first time he noticed them was when they suddenly appeared, one on each side of him.

Recovering quickly, Preacher smiled at them. "Good evening, ladies," he said.

"Good evening," they replied.

"Nice view from here," Preacher said, struggling hard to make some small talk. Truth to be told, he was uncomfortable in situations like this.

"Yes, quite lovely," one of the two girls replied.

"The captain said you are called Preacher," the other one said.

"But he also said that you aren't really a preacher," the first added.

"That's true," Preacher said. He turned away from the shoreline, and leaned back against the rail as he spoke to the two pretty women.

"I'm Emma Purdy," one of the women said.

"And I'm Cynthia Cain."

Preacher nodded his head. "I'm pleased to meet you, ladies."

"If you aren't a preacher, why do they call you preacher?" Emma asked.

"It's just something that happened to me once," Preacher said.

"Oh, please, do tell."

"It's a long story."

"Well, it's a long time before we get to St. Louis," Cynthia reminded him.

Preacher laughed. "I guess it is at that," he said. "All right, here goes."

Preacher began telling of the time he had been a prisoner of the Blackfeet, with no chance of help or escape. From somewhere an idea formed in his head and he began to sermonize, speaking in the same singsong voice he had once heard used by an itinerant preacher on the waterfront in St. Louis. He preached like a born-again, water-baptized, true believer in the Lord Almighty.

"The Indians didn't understand what I was saying," Preacher said, "but they listened anyway, and I continued to preach all through the night.

"Come the next morning, I was still preaching, amazed that I still had the strength to do it."

"What were you preaching about?" Emma asked.

"To tell the truth, I almost didn't even know what I was saying myself, but I kept on talking, kept on preaching.

"I preached all through the rest of that morning without stopping. The people of the village, men, women, and children, gathered around to listen, although they didn't have the slightest idea what I was saying.

"Finally, the elders of the village held a council where they decided I was crazy. And maybe I was."

"What do you mean, maybe you were? Do you think you were crazy?" Cynthia asked.

Preacher chuckled. "Well, I might have been a little crazy at the time. I don't know," he admitted. "But here's the thing. The Indians think that anyone who is crazy is touched by the Great Spirit. They're afraid to do any harm to him, because they don't want to offend the Great Spirit.

"So, the next thing you know, a couple of the old chiefs came over to me and untied me. And let me tell you, they didn't do it a moment too soon, because by then my mouth was parched and sore, and my vision was so blurred I could barely see. I don't think I could've lasted more than another five or ten minutes."

"And they just let you go?" Emma asked.

Preacher nodded. "Yes," he said.

"Oh, what a wonderful story!" Cynthia said.


The brothers Rance and Leon, scions of Angus Culpepper, owner of Culpepper Stage and Freight Lines, were making the trip to St. Louis on the same boat. Because they, like Emma Purdy and Cynthia Cain, were occupying first-class accommodations, they considered the two young ladies to be their exclusive property by right of social position.

Rance and Leon stood for a while at the rail, smoking their pipes and looking toward the flora and fauna of the riverbank as it slid past the boat. While there, they couldn't help but overhear the story Preacher told the two young women. Now, walking toward the stern of the boat, they were engaged in a private discussion about the man called Preacher.

"What a lout," Leon said. "No doubt, this is the longest conversation that creature has ever had with any woman who wasn't a whore."

"Probably even including his own mother," Rance replied.

"Do you mean he hasn't had a long conversation with her? Or do you mean that she is a whore?" Leon asked.

"He hasn't had a long conversation with her," Rance replied. Then he added, "And she probably is a whore."

Leon and Rance both laughed, though their laugh was brittle, like the shattering of crystal.

"You have to admit, that was some story he told," Leon said. "Do you believe it was true?"

"No. Mountain men are know to be great story-tellers. And liars."

"He had the ladies hanging on every word."

"Yes, unfortunately, he did," Rance said. "But it is obviously a story of self-aggrandizement, de-signed to make himself a hero in their eyes."

"What I don't understand is why Miss Purdy and Miss Cain would allow him to talk to them in the first place," Leon added. "He is traveling steerage, and one wonders where he even got the money for that."

"He is taking advantage of their innocence," Rance answered. "And I am personally offended by that."

"Mountain men are barely civilized; they spend months at a time with no company other than bears," Leon said.

"And no doubt, the bears find the presence of such men to be an affront to their dignity," Rance added. Again, the two young men laughed brittlely.

"He obviously has no sense of his proper place," Leon said.

Rance smiled. "Perhaps, before we reach St. Louis, we should teach him some manners."

"Yes," Leon said enthusiastically. "But let's not hurry. If we are patient and observant, I am positive that the opportunity will present itself."

The *Missouri Belle* carried two very long poles, called spars, at the bow of the boat. Whenever the boat got stuck on a sandbar, which was fairly often in the transit of a shallow river like the Missouri, those two poles would be put down to the river bottom at about a forty-five-degree angle. Then they were driven back by cables attached to a steam capstan. The result was a very powerful poling of the boat. That action was technically known as sparring, though as the poles looked like grasshopper legs when in the water, it was often referred to as "grasshoppering."

When they were four days out of Kansas City, they got stuck on a sandbar. It wasn't a bar they had blundered onto as a result of poor piloting, but a bar that covered the entire channel—and thus could not be avoided. Now their only hope lay in attempting to traverse the sandbar at its most advantageous part.

The poles dug into the river bottom, then strained and bent slightly. The boat crept forward, creaking and groaning under the exertion. Finally, the poles became extended and the boat could go no further. The poles would have to be retracted and the operation repeated.

Though Preacher had offered his help, the captain had explained that the best thing any of the passengers could do was stay out of the way, and now Preacher was accommodating him on that request.

The poles were reset, and the operation started a second time. Again, the poles strained backward, and again the boat started sliding forward. The poles bent as before, but suddenly one of the cables snapped, and it whipped back around with a loud whoosh.

"Look out!" Preacher shouted and he dove toward Emma and Cynthia, taking them both down. The cable whizzed by over them and smashed through the flagpole, breaking it as cleanly as if it were no more than a matchstick.

The operator of the capstan also dove to the deck just in time to avoid it, but because the capstan was still running, the cable continued to whip around, flaying and smashing everything in its path. The operator could not stand up because the cable was whipping over his head, which also meant he couldn't get to the throttle lever to shut down the capstan. As long as the capstan turned, the cable would continue to whirl about madly.

"We've got to get that engine shut down!" the captain shouted. "If that cable flies loose and hits the boiler, we are going to have one hell of an explosion!"

The cable continued to whirl about, but as some

of the steam pressure was vented off, it wasn't whirling quite as fast as it had at the beginning. That was little consolation, though, because it was still moving with enough force to make a shambles out of the bow deck. It took down the flagpole with its first revolution, then it smashed through the railing, and now the operator was still trapped beneath the slashing line.

Preacher watched it spin for two more revolutions. When he had it timed just right, he leaped up, ran to the bow deck, ducked at just the right moment, and reached the engine lever. He pushed it shut. The cable, without the whirling momentum of the capstan, fell whistling into the river.

"Great job, lad!" the captain said, congratulating him, and the rest of the passengers and crew applauded him.

"You saved our lives," Emma said.

"That would have killed us if you hadn't gotten us out of the way," Cynthia added.

"Don't forget, I was saving my life too," Preacher said modestly.

Preacher's heroism had elevated him, not only in the opinion of the two young women, but in the eyes of the passengers and crew as well. For the Culpepper brothers, though, it just made them more determined to take care of him before they reached St. Louis.

That opportunity came on the last night before they were to reach St. Louis. Leon and Rance came out of the grand salon, where they had been gambling and had had a run of bad luck.

"I lost twenty dollars," Leon said. "How about you?"

"Thirty-five dollars," Rance replied.

"I know that gambler is cheating," Leon said. "But he is too good. I couldn't catch him at it."

"Yeah, I never saw such bad luck," Rance said. They had stepped out to the rail to get a breath of air, when suddenly Rance stuck his hand out to keep his brother from advancing any farther. "Brother, I think perhaps our luck is about to change," he said quietly.

"What do you mean?"

"Look."

Rance pointed to the stern of the boat. There, curled up next to a stanchion, they saw Preacher. It was obvious that he was sound asleep.

"You know what would be funny?" Rance said.

"What's that?"

"I think it would be really funny if we just sort of, quietly walked back there and rolled that son of a bitch off the boat. He'd be three feet underwater before he knew what happened to him."

"Brother, you are a genius," Leon said.

Moving quietly, and staying in the shadows, the two men crept to the back of the boat.

One of the side-mounted paddle wheels jerked out of sequence as they often did, and it caused the boat to make a sideways lurch. It splashed a little water onto Preacher, and he opened his eyes. Just before he closed them again, he saw Leon and Rance Culpepper slipping through the shadows toward him.

He wasn't sure what they were up to, but they had already let him know that they considered his friendliness toward the two women to be above his station. He was fairly certain that, whatever the plan, they were up to no good.

Leon and Rance moved out of the shadows, then covered the open space between the after cabin and the stern of the boat. Leaning forward, they stuck their arms out, intending to roll Preacher over the side of the boat.

Preacher timed it just right, reaching up and grabbing their arms just as they were leaning forward. With their forward momentum already established, it was a simple maneuver for him to pull them past him. Shouting in alarm and surprise, both Leon and Rance tumbled overboard.

Preacher stood up and looked back into the churning wake, where he saw both heads pop up. The two brothers shouted, but the boat was making so much noise that, even to Preacher's ears, their shouts were barely audible. Preacher looked around to see if anyone else had seen them go overboard, but nobody appeared to have done so.

He watched the brothers swim toward the bank. Reaching the shallow part of the river, they stood up. Turning, they shook their fists angrily at him. Preacher saw a couple of farmhouses nearby, so he knew the brothers weren't in any mortal danger from being stranded there, but they would have a long walk into St. Louis. With a little laugh, he rubbed his hands together, then lay down again and went back to sleep.

As they approached St. Louis from the river, Preacher marveled at the changes the city had undergone since he had first laid eyes on it. He had come to St. Louis the first time in 1813, and from there, he had joined a regiment of volunteers to fight against the British at the Battle of New Orleans.

Even though Preacher was only fourteen years old, he had been breveted a lieutenant in that battle, earning the respect of his commanders and the men who had served with him. Since that time, Missouri had become a state, and St. Louis had grown from a frontier town to a bustling, prosperous city of nearly twenty thousand people. That was a lot of people—too many people for someone like Art, who had grown accustomed to life in the wilderness and went for days or weeks without seeing another human soul.

St. Louis was a vibrant city, alive with the pulse of commerce and enterprise: the scream of a steam-powered sawmill, the sound of steamboat whistles from the river, the hiss and boom of boats' engines, and the clatter of wagons rolling across cobblestone streets. To someone used to solitude so complete that he could hear the flutter of a bird's wings, the noise of civilization was almost unbearable.

Preacher had not planned to visit St. Louis during this trip down from the mountains, and had in fact not planned on any visit in the near future. But, upon learning that his dear Jennie had been murdered, he'd felt that he had no choice. He had to come, to find out just what happened, and to find justice for her.

"I say, Preacher," the purser said, coming to him shortly after the boat docked. "I seem to have lost the Culpepper brothers. Have you seen them recently?"

"Yes," Preacher said.

"Where are they?"

"Oh, they got off the boat last night," Preacher said without further explanation.

"They got off last night? My word," the purser said, scratching his head as he started back to his office.

Emma and Cynthia came to the deck of the boat, preparing to leave. They were accompanied by the headmistress of the finishing school they were to attend, and followed by three young black boys who were struggling to carry their luggage.

"Oh, Miss Peabody, this is Preacher," Emma said by way of introduction.

Miss Peabody held her glasses up on a long stem and looked at Preacher. Seeing by his dress that he was a frontiersman, she turned away from him without even acknowledging his presence.

"Come, ladies, we mustn't tarry," she said.

"He saved our lives," Cynthia said.

Miss Peabody hesitated for a moment, then turned to Preacher. "I'm sure the families of these young ladies would be more than willing to provide you with a reward for your service," she said.

Preacher nodded. "Thank you, ma'am, but seeing their pretty smiles is reward enough."

Both women giggled in delight, but Miss Peabody just let out a disapproving "hurrumph" and, again, ordered the girls to come with her.

Preacher watched them get into a beautifully lacquered carriage, then drive away. He picked up the roll he kept his own gear in, tossed it over his shoulder, walked down the gangplank and up the street.

A neatly painted sign on front of the building read: FURS BOUGHT AND SOLD, WILLIAM ASHLEY, PROP. Squaring his shoulders, Preacher went inside.

A little bell hanging from the door summoned the proprietor from the back. A tall, rather dignified-looking man came up to greet him. Then, recognizing Preacher, he smiled broadly and extended his hand.

"Preacher!" he said. "If you aren't a sight for sore eyes."

"Hello, Mr. Ashley," Preacher said, returning the handshake. "It's good to see you again."

Ashley leaned over to see beyond Preacher. "Did you bring your own plews?"

"No, no, I sold them to your representative out at the Rendezvous."

"Oh? Well, then, what brings you to St. Louis? Not that I'm not pleased to see you," he added quickly.

Preacher pulled the letter from inside his shirt. "I came because of this," he said.

The smile left Ashley's face, and he nodded. "About Miss Jennie," he said.

"Yes."

"To tell the truth, I rather suspected that would bring you to St. Louis."

"I would like to visit Jennie's grave," Preacher said. "Is it marked?"

"Yes, I put up a marker for her."

"Thanks. Where in the cemetery will I find her grave?"

"I don't even need to tell you that. You'll find her easily enough," Ashley said.

Preacher looked puzzled. "What do you mean?"

"The cemetery is just down at the end of the street here. Go on down there and look for yourself. You'll see what I'm talking about," he said mysteriously.

"May I leave this here?" Preacher asked, taking the roll from his shoulder.

"Yes, of course," Ashley said, taking the roll from Preacher and putting it down behind the counter. "Go visit Jennie's grave, then come on back. We'll have dinner at Chardonnay's."

"Thanks."

Leaving the shop, Preacher started down the street toward the cemetery, wondering what Ashley meant when he said he wouldn't have any problem locating Jennie's grave.

As soon as Preacher reached the gate to the cemetery, he saw what Ashley was talking about. There, on the far side of the cemetery under a spreading maple tree, he saw a familiar-looking dog lying on one of the graves.

"Dog?" Preacher called.

Dog raised his head. Then, seeing Preacher, he bounded across the cemetery toward him. Preacher dropped down on one knee. When Dog reached him, Preacher began rubbing him on the head and behind his ears, one of which, he noticed, was only half an ear. In addition, there were half-a-dozen scars on the dog's head and body.

"Is that Jennie's grave over there?" Preacher asked.

Whether in sorrow or shame for having failed in his duty, Dog lowered his head.

"I'm not accusing you, Dog," Preacher said quietly. "From the looks of you, you did all that you could. Come on, take me to see Jennie."

With Dog leading the way, Preacher followed through the cemetery until he reached Jennie's grave. Dog lay down. Putting his nose between his paws, he looked up at Preacher, sharing his grief.

Preacher read the inscription:

*Precious Flower,*
*Divine providence hath seen fit to pluck thee*
*from this earth*
*and transplant thee to the garden of Eden*
*where a more fitting abode awaits thee.*
*Cherished one,*
*As long as blood flows through the veins*
*of the hand that pens these lines,*
*Thy memory shall be kept ever green.*
*Gone but not forgotten,*
*Carla*

# EIGHT

"You found Dog, I see," Ashley said when Preacher returned with the dog several minutes later.

Preacher sat in a chair, tipped it back against the wall, and began rubbing Dog behind his ears.

"Yes," he said.

"Did you see the inscription on the tombstone?"

"I saw it."

"Carla had me put it there. You remember her, don't you? She was one of Jennie's girls, but not really one of her girls. Carla never was a whore."

"Yes, I remember her. She's what now, sixteen, seventeen?"

Ashley laughed. "She's twenty-two now, and quite a pretty woman. She's waitin' tables down at Little Man's Café."

"Mr. Ashley . . ."

"Lord, Preacher, haven't we known each other long enough for you to call me Bill?"

"Bill," Preacher said, "you said you thought Ben Caviness was one of those who killed Jennie?"

"That's right. Nobody saw who did it, but if I had to make a guess, he's the one I would pick."

"In the letter you said there were two of them, but only one got away."

"Yep."

"What about the one that was caught? Haven't you been able to make him say anything?"

"If he does say something, he'll be saying it to God," Ashley said. "We found him at the same time we found Miss Jennie. He's dead."

"Dead? How? What happened to him?"

Ashley nodded toward Dog, who was now sleeping with his head resting on Preacher's foot. "As near as we can figure it, Dog killed him," he said. "I mean, Dog must've put up one hell of a fight."

"If nobody saw it, and you found one man dead, how do you even know there was another one?"

"Because when we found Dog, he was more dead than alive," Ashley said. "And he had a man's ear clenched in his teeth."

"An ear?"

"Yep. And that ear didn't come off the dead man, 'cause he still had both his ears. That means there was another person involved."

"Speaking of ears, I notice that Dog just barely has both of his," Preacher said. "He also seems to have several scars."

"Like I said, Dog was more dead than alive when we found him. We really didn't think he was going to live," Ashley said. "He had a gunshot wound, and six stab wounds. He was lying in a pool of blood, though most of it was Jennie's blood. He was lying on her body when we found him."

"What was his name? The fella who was killed, I mean. Do you know?"

"They called him Slater, but nobody knows if that was his first name or his last. He drifted in here about a year ago. Some say he had been a river pirate; others say he was just a petty thief. He was almost always in some kind of trouble, I know that. Folks all agree that Dog did the city a favor by killing him."

"I suppose," Preacher replied. "But it would've been good to talk to him, to find out for sure if Caviness was the other man."

"Well, whether it was Caviness or not, whoever did it is not in St. Louis," Ashley said. "We know that much at least."

"How do we know that?"

"Because everyone in this town is wearin' both their ears," Ashley replied with a little laugh.

The men were quiet for a moment. Then Ashley nodded toward the dog. "I have to tell you, I'm surprised to see him here," he said.

"Why is that?"

"Because this is the first time since the day Miss Jennie was buried that Dog has left the cemetery. Folks have taken notice of him, and someone is always bringing him something to eat, just because they want to. There are a lot of rabbits and squirrels out there, and Dog is pretty resourceful. There is also a stream that runs through the place."

"I wonder why he won't leave the cemetery," Preacher said.

"Oh, I don't think that's all that much of a

mystery," Ashley replied. "You did leave him to look out for Miss Jennie, didn't you?"

"Yes."

"I think he's feeling guilty for not being able to do what you asked."

"I'll be damned," Preacher said. "You might be right." He looked down at Dog. "Dog?"

Dog opened his eyes and looked up at him.

"Dog, you don't have anything to feel guilty about," Preacher said. "You did the best you could do. You killed one of them, and you fixed it so that when I find the other one, I will recognize him." He reached down and rubbed Dog on the head again. "You did a good job, Dog, and I am very proud of you."

Dog stretched, stood up, then shook himself so that the loose skin slipped around noisily. He licked Preacher's hand.

Ashley laughed. "You know what? I think you just took a big load off his mind. I really do think he was worried about what you would think of him failing his responsibility."

"He didn't fail anything," Preacher said.

"Nevertheless, I bet he won't spend all of his time down at the cemetery anymore."

"Listen, didn't you say something about buying my dinner?"

"I did. Chardonnay's is just down the street. That's the best restaurant in St. Louis."

"Yes, I've eaten there," Preacher said. "But if it's all the same to you, I believe I'd just as soon eat at—where is it you said Carla works?"

"Little Man's."

"Yes. Let's eat at Little Man's," Preacher said.

"Preacher!" Carla squealed in joy when Preacher and Ashley stepped into Little Man's Café. She was carrying a pitcher of water and she put it down, hurrying over to give Preacher a big hug.

Preacher returned her hug, and she hung onto him for a long time. After a moment, he felt a wetness on his cheek and realized that she was crying. He didn't force her away from him, but let her hold him for as long as she wished. Finally, she drew away and, raising the end of her apron, dabbed at her tear-filled eyes.

"You know about Jennie?" she asked.

Preacher nodded. "Mr. Ashley sent me a letter. I just visited her grave. That was really nice, Carla, what you had put on her tombstone."

"Jennie was like a big sister to me," Carla said. "I've never loved any person like I loved her. She loved me too." She smiled through her tears. "But of course, she didn't love me the way she loved you. She was really in love with you, Preacher, did you know that?"

Preacher nodded. "Yes," he said. "I knew it."

"It wasn't all one-sided, was it? You did love her too, didn't you? I mean, I know you did."

"It wasn't one-sided," Preacher said. "I did love her, perhaps even more than I thought I did. But nothing would have ever worked out between us."

"I guess not. Oh, if you visited her grave, then you saw Dog there. He won't leave it, you know."

"He won't?" Ashley asked with a broad smile. He nodded toward the front door. "Who do you think that is?"

Looking in the direction Ashley indicated, Carla saw Dog curled up on the front porch. She gasped and put her hand to her mouth. "Oh, my," she said. "There he is, on the front porch."

"Yes."

"But I don't understand. Ever since Jennie died, day or night, rain or shine, cold weather or hot, Dog has been right down there, lying on Jennie's grave. He never leaves the cemetery, never. Yet there he is, right outside on the front porch."

"I released him," Preacher said.

"You released him? What do you mean?"

"I had charged Dog with looking out for Jennie. He thought he had failed."

"Preacher told him he did all he could do to protect Miss Jennie," Ashley said.

"But I told him that," Carla said. "We've all told him that."

"Yes, but you weren't the one who charged him with that responsibility," Preacher said. "Only I did that, and in Dog's mind, only I could release him from that charge."

"Bless his heart," Carla said. "Maybe he can find peace now."

Lying out on the porch, Dog looked through the door at Bear Killer and the friend of Bear Killer's woman. Dog had believed that Bear Killer would be angry with him because he had not done his job.

He had tried as hard as he could, and even now, he could recall the warm rush of blood as he ripped open the neck of one of the two men who had attacked Jennie. Even as he was engaged with that one, the one Bear Killer's woman called Caviness was attacking him with a knife, stabbing him repeatedly.

When Dog felt the life drain from the one he had attacked, he turned on Caviness, despite the pain and the weakness he was feeling. He went for Caviness's neck, but Caviness covered it with his arm, and turned his head to one side. Dog ripped off his ear, and heard Caviness scream in pain.

Then Dog saw a flash of light and heard a loud noise. He felt a blow to his side, followed by a darkness. When he came to, he saw that Bear Killer's woman was dead, lying in a pool of blood from a wound in her neck.

Dog felt an intense shame for having failed in his duty. Bear Killer had asked him to protect his woman, and he hadn't done so. He could not bring himself to leave her, even when she was buried. He stayed at the place where they buried her, determined to carry out the responsibility Bear Killer had given him, determined to continue to protect her, even though she was now dead.

But now, Bear Killer had returned. Dog could see that Bear Killer wasn't angry. Bear Killer understood that Dog had done all he could. Dog was at peace.

*\*\*\**

Ordinarily, the hotel would not allow dogs in the patrons' rooms. But like nearly everyone else in town, the proprietor of the Dunn Hotel knew the story of Dog, how he had killed one of the men who attacked his mistress and had chewed the ear off the other. He also knew that Dog had stayed at Jennie's grave all this time, out of a sense of loyalty, or love, or responsibility that was almost human-like. Because of that, when Preacher took a room that night, and walked up the stairs with Dog following right behind, the proprietor said nothing.

In fact, he thought, both Preacher and the dog were fast becoming legends. It might well be that being able to say they stayed in his hotel would mean an increase in business.

Preacher and Dog stepped into the magistrate's office the next morning to find Constable Billings sitting in a chair with his feet propped up on his desk. He was paring an apple, and one long peel hung from it all the way to the floor. He looked up as Preacher came in.

"I remember you," the constable said. "You're the one they call Preacher."

"Yes."

"I expect you're here to ask about Miss Jennie. William Ashley said she was your woman."

"She was."

Billings finished, then tossed the peeled apple to

Preacher. "Want this?" he asked. "I don't particularly like apples."

Preacher looked at Billings with a confused expression on his face.

"If you don't like apples, why did you peel it?"

"For the peel," Billings replied. He stretched the long, unbroken peel out on the floor. "How long you reckon that is?"

"I don't know. Three, four feet maybe?"

Billings stroked his chin. "Yeah, that's pretty much what it looks like to me as well." He sighed, picked up the peel, then opened the door to the little potbellied stove and tossed it in. "That's not long enough."

"I beg your pardon?"

"That's not long enough," Billings repeated. "You see, I've got me a two-dollar bet with the mayor of the town on who can make the longest unbroken apple peel. He claims he can do five feet. We're all set to do it come Saturday."

"About Jennie," Preacher said.

"We found her down by the riverside. Her throat was cut, but before that, it looked like she had been beat up pretty bad.

"Found Slater there too. His throat was ripped out. Figure Miss Jennie's dog did that. The dog was still guarding her. We had the devil's own time getting to her. I reckon the dog finally decided that we didn't mean her any harm."

"Mr. Ashley said there was a second man. A fella by the name of Ben Caviness."

"Well, now, we don't know for sure that that's who

it was," Billings said. "I reckon Ashley told you the dog had a man's ear clinched in his teeth. Funny that he didn't eat it. It was almost like he wanted us to know there was someone else."

"Mr. Ashley seems pretty sure it was Caviness."

"Well, some folks did see Caviness and Slater together on the night it happened," Constable Billings said.

"All right. If you know that, how come you won't say for sure that the one who got away was Caviness?"

" 'Cause we don't have no actual witnesses to the killin', 'cept for that dog there," Billings said, pointing to Dog. He chuckled. "And it's kind of hard to identify someone by his ear."

"Do you still have it?"

"Have what? The ear?"

"Yes. Do you still have it?"

"Now, just what in the Sam Hill makes you think I'd hang onto somethin' like that?"

"Do you still have it?" Preacher asked again.

Billings sighed, then walked over to a chest and pulled out a drawer. "As a matter of fact, I do," he said. "I dried it out in the sun, so it wouldn't rot away."

"I'd like it, please."

"What are you aimin' to do with it?"

"As soon as I find Caviness, I aim to sew this ear back on his head," Preacher said. "Then I aim to kill him."

"Sounds reasonable enough," Billings said, handing the sun-blackened piece of leather to

Preacher. "Oh, you might want this as well." He took an envelope from the drawer.

"What is that?"

"It's everything I've got on Miss Jennie: complaints she made, and complaints made against her. I don't know that it'll do you any good, but I got no need to be keepin' it now, so it's yours if you want it."

"Thanks." Preacher said, taking the envelope, then starting toward the door.

"Preacher?"

Preacher was nearly to the door when the constable called him. Stopping, he turned toward Billings.

"Yes?"

"The man you're lookin' for, whether it's Caviness or someone else, ain't in St. Louis. I'm pretty sure about that. If he is here and you find him and kill him, well, I just want you to know you won't be havin' no trouble with me or the law, seein' as any son of a bitch who would do somethin' like that needs killin' pure and simple. But if you find him in some other town, and you kill him there, then you might have some explainin' to do."

"I know," Preacher said.

"What I'm sayin' is, once you leave St. Louis, there won't be nothin' I can do to help you."

"I know," Preacher said again.

"Just so's you understand."

Preacher nodded, then stepped outside. Dog followed Preacher as he headed toward La-Barge's Tavern.

***

In the shadowed interior of the tavern, Preacher ordered a beer, then sat at a table in the back. Dog curled himself onto the floor beside Preacher's chair.

"Folks don't normally bring dogs into the saloon," the barkeep said.

"You want him out, you run him out," Preacher replied.

"You," the bartender said to Dog. He pointed to the door. "Out! No dogs allowed in here."

Dog made no effort to respond.

The bartender came around from behind the bar. "I said get out of here," he said menacingly. He took a couple of steps toward Dog, but stopped when the hackles went up on Dog's neck. Dog bared his teeth and growled a low, quiet, but menacing growl.

The bartender stopped. "I, uh, guess you can stay," he said, retreating back to the bar. Dog closed his eyes in dismissal.

Preacher had paid no attention to what was going on between Dog and the bartender. Instead, he busied himself with dumping the contents of the envelope.

Examining the little pile on his table, Preacher found a document written in Jennie's neat hand.

*I, Jennie (no middle name, no last name), do hereby file this complaint against Mr. Ben Caviness.*

*Last night, while returning home from a job*

*I was doing for Mrs. Sybil Abernathy, Mr. Ben*
*Caviness jumped out of an alley in front of me.*
*I believe it was his intention to attack me, but*
*my dog ran him off.*

There was also a complaint filed against the
River Bank of St. Louis, and Theodore Epson, for
failing to credit her mortgage payment.

In addition, there were several documents that had
been filed against Jennie. These were much older, the
oldest being six years old, the newest one almost two
years old. All of these had been filed by Mrs. Sybil
Abernathy. The gist of Mrs. Abernathy's complaints
was that Jennie was a prostitute and the practice of
her profession prevented St. Louis from realizing its
potential as a city of culture and influence.

There was also a letter in the file from Theodore
Epson, responding to an inquiry made by Constable
Billings.

*Mr. Theodore Epson*
*Chief Teller*
*Trust Bank of Philadelphia*

*Dear Constable Billings:*
*I assure you, sir, that any suspicion you may*
*have that I absconded with cash due the bank*
*is totally without merit. The woman in ques-*
*tion, known only as Jennie, was indeed in debt*
*to the River Bank of St. Louis for the mortgage*
*held on her home.*
*In point of fact her home was not a private*

*residence as she claimed in her loan application. It was, instead, used as a house of ill repute. Thus, you can see that if a case of fraud is to be made, it should rightfully be made against her, for misrepresenting herself in securing the loan.*

*I cannot believe that anyone would take seriously the accusations of a whore against a respectable banker.*

*Sincerely,*
*Theodore Epson*

"Preacher?"

It was a woman's voice and, looking up, Preacher saw Carla coming toward him. Generally, only bar girls and women of the street, plying their profession, would enter a saloon. But Carla was very much at ease in LaBarge's Tavern. She was not, and had never been a prostitute, but in her younger days she had worked as a bar girl in this very establishment.

"Carla," Preacher replied. Preacher was a man of the mountains, but he retained enough manners to stand as she approached his table. "What are you doing here?"

"I thought I would . . . well . . . I mean, if you don't have other plans, I thought I might cook supper for you," Carla said.

"Cook supper for me where?" Preacher asked.

"Jennie and I shared a small house over on Olive," she said. "Well, actually, in the alley behind Olive. I'd be happy to cook dinner for you tonight."

"You don't have to cook for me, Carla. We could have dinner at Little Man's."

Carla smiled. "I work at Little Man's," she said. "Sometimes I just want to get out of there."

"Oh, yes, well, I guess I can understand that. All right, how about if we have dinner at Chardonnay's?"

"Why, Preacher, one would think you don't want my home cooking," Carla said with a teasing pout.

"No, no, nothing like that," Preacher replied. "I'm just trying to keep you from going to any trouble for me, that's all."

"You don't know anything about women, do you, Preacher?"

Preacher smiled, and shook his head. "Not much," he admitted.

"Sometimes, women want to go to the trouble of fixing dinner."

"All right, if you put it that way. I'll be glad to come."

"About seven?"

"Seven will be fine," Preacher agreed.

# NINE

After leaping off the boat, Caviness managed to swim ashore, though he nearly drowned in the process. He lay on the riverbank for several minutes, trying to get his breath back. Caviness had not considered the fact that someone might be looking for him. No one saw him kill Jennie, so how would they know it was him?

Finally, Caviness stood and hitched up his pants. When he did, he suddenly realized that he had lost his knife. Then, he discovered he had lost all of his money as well. He looked back toward the river. Evidently, it had fallen from his pocket when he jumped into the water.

The money was in bills, issued by the Bank of the United States. It was paper money, not coin, which meant that the money was probably scattered all down the river by now.

"Son of a bitch!" Caviness screamed at the top of his voice. "Son of a bitch, son of a bitch, son of a bitch!"

Caviness crawled up to the top of the bank. From

there he could see the boat moving majestically downriver, its chimneys belching smoke, the paddles slapping into the water, churning a wake that followed behind.

He had no real idea where he was, and he was wet, cold, hungry, and broke. Now he had to get to Philadelphia. He began following the river south.

That night, he saw a flatboat that had put in for the night. There were two men operating the boat, and he watched as they made it fast, then built a fire for their supper. The smell of the food made his stomach growl, but he stayed hidden until both were asleep. Then, sneaking down to the boat, he slipped the rope from the tree and pushed out into the stream. The current caught him and started him downriver at a fairly good clip.

All that night and the next day he rode the boat downriver. He passed Cape Girardeau, because he knew the steamboat was going to stop there and he was afraid they might know about him. The next town south was the small town of Commerce, so he put in there.

Commerce consisted of no more than a dozen buildings, all parallel with the river's edge. When he landed, a man came down to take the rope and make the boat fast for him.

"Howdy. The name is Ferrell. I own a store here. What is it you are carrying?"

"Axes, shovels, iron stoves," Caviness replied. He had examined the cargo during the trip down.

"Are you looking to sell it here? Or do you plan on going down to New Madrid?" Ferrell asked.

"I'll sell it here."

"Because you know I can't pay as much as they do down at New Madrid."

"What can you pay me?"

"Well, let me take a look here," Ferrell said.

All the while Ferrell was poking through the cargo, he kept glancing up at Caviness. Caviness knew that he was looking at the wound left by the missing ear. Had the boat stopped here as well? Did this man know who he was? Finally, he could take it no longer.

"What the hell are you looking at, mister?" he demanded, angrily.

"I'm sorry," Ferrell said, looking away quickly. "I know it ain't good manners to stare at somethin' like that. I was just wonderin' how you come by a wound like that."

"I was bit by a bear," Caviness replied, sticking to his original story.

"I'm sorry I was starin' at you," Ferrell said, apologizing again. "I know it's rude, I just . . . " He let the sentence die.

"How much will you give me for all this?" Caviness asked.

"I figure I can pay you one hundred dollars," the man said. "Like I said, you'd probably get more for it down in New Madrid, but I'll give you a hundred for it."

"I'll take it," Caviness said, smiling broadly. What a stroke of luck! This would replace the money he lost when he jumped into the river.

"All right, just bring your bill of lading on up to

my store and I'll pay you," Ferrell said, stepping off the boat and heading toward the scattering of buildings.

"Bill of lading? I don't have no bill of lading."

Ferrell looked back in surprise. "You don't have a bill of lading?"

"No," Caviness replied. In truth, he didn't know if he had one or not, because he wasn't even sure of what it was.

"Mister, how'd you come by those goods if you don't have a bill of lading?"

"I won the boat and everything on it in a card game," Caviness answered.

Ferrell looked at him suspiciously. "Where?"

"Up in Ste. Genevieve," Caviness said. "If you'll just give me the one hundred dollars, I'll be on my way."

"Can't do that," Ferrell replied.

"What do you mean you can't? Why not?"

"Mister, you may not know this, but time was when we had river pirates somethin' awful. They're most cleaned out now, but ever' now and then there's outlaws will prey on the boats comin' downriver. So now it's a law. Anything we buy off a boat has to have a bill of lading. If you don't have one, I can't buy your goods."

"I'll sell it all to you for fifty dollars," Caviness said, watching the money he thought he had slipping away from him.

"Mister, I wouldn't give you twenty-five dollars for it. Like as not, the man you won it from stole it off somebody."

Ferrell walked away from the boat.

"Ten dollars!" Caviness shouted. "You can have the whole load for ten dollars!"

Ferrell stopped, then looked back toward Caviness. "Mister, I'm going to get the constable. He might want to talk to you about that man you won that from."

Caviness had no desire to talk to the constable, so as Ferrell walked away, he slipped the rope free and pushed back into the stream. He reached the confluence of the Mississippi and Ohio the next afternoon, and there he abandoned the boat on the Illinois side.

From there he started following the Ohio River. About every other day or so, he would see boats going upriver, but he was afraid to take passage on one of them, for fear they might be looking for him.

If it hadn't been for that damn dog chewing off his ear, he could've boarded any of the boats and no one would have been any the wiser. But if they were looking for someone with a chewed-off ear, that would make it pretty hard for him to blend in.

He wasn't sure if the news had spread to the small towns along the river, but there was a good chance that it had. After all, the boats were making better time than he was, and news like that was generally the first thing folks would talk about.

When he abandoned the boat, he took the rest of the food with him, but it ran out after a few days. He had one day of absolute hunger, then happened onto a field of potatoes and dug up several of them. Those sustained him for the next several days. Then he was drawn to a travel camp by the smell of smoke from the fire.

Advancing just to the edge of the golden bubble of light, Caviness stayed in the darkness. That way, he could see but not be seen.

There was only one man in the camp, an older man from the looks of his white hair and beard. The man had no idea that he was being examined, but the horse sensed the presence of a stranger and began whickering. Alerted, the man looked up.

"Hello?" he said. "Anyone out there?"

"Hello the camp," Caviness called. "Can I come in?"

"Sure," the man replied. "Come on in. I've got enough stew for two. I'd enjoy the company."

"Thanks," Caviness said, walking into the bubble of light.

"You got your own pan?" the man asked.

"No."

"No matter, we can get a piece of bark to use as a plate. Have a . . . God's name, man! What happened to your ear?"

"I had a run-in with a bear."

"Bear? In Ohio?"

"Back in Missouri," Caviness said.

"Oh, my, you were lucky to survive," the man said. Finding a flat piece of birch bark, he spooned up some of the stew, then handed it over to Caviness. "I don't reckon you have a fork or a spoon either," he said.

"No," Caviness replied. "But this'll do." He

held up a smaller piece of bark and began using it as a spoon.

"If you don't mind my asking, how is it that you are traveling with none of the things you need?"

"I was traveling by boat," Caviness said. "The boat sank and I lost everything."

"Oh. I'm sorry to hear that. Where are you headed?"

"Philadelphia."

"Big town, Philadelphia," the man replied. "My name is Seagraves. Milton Seagraves. I'm on my way to Cincinnati to take a job with a newspaper. What's your line of work?"

"Whatever I can get," Caviness said. "I'm sort of a handyman."

"Well, if you are willing to work, I'm sure there'll be plenty of jobs for you in a city as big as Philadelphia."

"You aren't carrying a gun?"

"A gun?" Seagraves replied. He shook his head. "Heavens, no, why should I carry a gun? Ohio is civilized country."

"I just thought you might have one," Caviness said.

"No, siree, I don't own one and I don't intend to ever own one. I don't hold much with guns. I do have a knife, though," he said, pulling the knife from his belt. It was a good-sized knife, much like the one Caviness had used to kill Jennie, and the one he had lost in the river.

"Good stew," Caviness said. "I appreciate the invite."

"You're mighty welcome. Like I said, I enjoy the company."

"Fire's getting' low," Caviness said.

"That's all right. Bout time to turn in anyway."

"I see a good-sized piece of wood over there," Caviness said. "I'll get it and throw just one more piece on the fire."

Seagraves chuckled. "Go ahead. If we're going to talk a while longer, we may as well be lookin' at each other while we're doin' it."

Caviness walked over to pick up the piece of wood. It was about three feet long and three or four inches in diameter. In truth, it wasn't a very good piece for burning at all, but it was an excellent piece for Caviness's use.

"So tell me about that bear," Seagraves said without turning toward Caviness, who was now coming up behind Seagraves's back. "How did he happen to chaw off an ear without taking off your head?" He chuckled. "That's a story I'd like to—"

That was as far as Seagraves got. At that moment, Caviness brought the club around, holding it in both hands and swinging hard. The blow crushed the side of Seagraves's head, and he fell forward into the fire.

The next morning Seagraves was still belly-down, with his head in the ashes of what had been the previous night's fire. His head was turned to one side and the bottom of his face was burned away so that what flesh was left was blackened and disfigured. Amazingly, the top half of his face was undamaged.

Caviness found a change of clothes that were

somewhat less conspicuous than the clothes he was wearing, so he changed. Then, saddling Seagrave's horse, he rode off.

## Near Alexandria, Ohio

Two days later, when he smelled pork chops frying, he determined to find its source. Riding through a cornfield, he came upon a small farmhouse, the origin of the enticing aroma. Dismounting, he tied the horse off, then using trees and bushes to mask his approach, eased up to the house.

Looking through the window, he saw a man sitting in a chair, smoking a pipe and reading a book. In addition to the man, there were two women standing at the stove. As he examined them more closely, he saw that one of the women was very young, perhaps no more than fifteen or sixteen years old.

"Papa, supper's about ready," the younger woman said.

"All right, missy, I'll sit at the table soon as I finish reading this page."

"Go get Billy, Suzie," the older woman said.

Nodding, Suzie opened the back door. From his position of observation through the window, Caviness saw that the man was sitting with his back to the door Suzie had just used. That was good. That meant that the door would be unlocked because Suzie had just gone through it. And as Suzie's father's back was to the door, Caviness would be able to sneak in without being seen.

Moving quietly, and with the knife he had taken from Seagraves in his hand, Caviness opened the door and slipped inside.

"Well, that didn't take long," the man said without looking around.

Caviness stepped up behind the chair, then drew the knife across the man's throat, cutting jugular and windpipe. Unable to make a sound, the man grabbed the wound on his neck, then tumbled forward from the chair.

The woman had stepped out of the kitchen for a moment, but hearing the fall, called out.

"Hiram, what was that? What just fell?"

Caviness stepped quickly to one side of the door and waited for the woman to come back into the room.

"Hiram?" the woman called again.

Once again, Caviness made use of his knife, slicing the woman's throat. She died as silently as her husband.

With the bloody knife still in his hand, Caviness walked over to the table, where he picked up a pork chop and began eating.

As soon as the girl came back, Caviness would take care of her . . . though not before he had a little fun with her. Then he would search the house for a gun, any money they might have, and some extra food. Maybe a blanket or a quilt would be nice too.

Outside the house, seventeen-year-old Billy Potter was using a pitchfork to toss hay in the feeding trough when Suzie came to get him.

"Mama says get washed up for supper."

"What are we having?"

"Pork chops," Suzie answered. "And I cooked them."

"Ha! If you cooked them, they are probably poison," Billy teased.

"Well, if you don't like them, you don't have to eat them."

"Oh, I'll eat them, all right," Billy said. "I won't like them, but I'll eat them."

Finishing with the hay, Billy walked over to the well, where he drew out some water and poured it into a basin.

"Billy, are you going to the county fair this Saturday?"

"Yes."

"Will you take me?" Suzie asked hopefully.

"No, I won't take you. Who wants to go to a county fair with a little sister hanging around him all the time?"

"Little sister?" Suzie replied. "I'm near as old as you are," Suzie said. "And I'm almost a woman, full grow'd now."

"Yeah, that's what I'm afraid of. You'll go sparking with all the boys, and I'm the one that will get in trouble for letting you do it."

"I won't."

"You will too. You're the biggest tease in the whole county."

"Ohh, you make me so mad!" Suzie said. She grabbed the pan of water and started to toss it on him.

"No, no, wait! You can go! I was just teasing!" Billy said, laughing.

"Promise?"

"I promise."

Suzie put the water pan down and Billy grabbed it. "I'll show you to threaten me," he said, starting after her.

Laughing and screaming, Suzie ran back up to the house with Billy chasing her.

"Mama! Billy is going to . . ." Suzie started, but as soon as she stepped into the house she gasped, then screamed.

There, on the floor of the kitchen, lay her mother and dad, both with their throats cut. The most terrifying-looking human being Suzie had ever seen was standing there over them, holding a bloody knife in one hand and a pork chop in the other.

Billy, coming in right behind her, saw the scene as well.

"Suzie, run!" Billy shouted, pulling her back outside and giving her a shove. Billy turned and ran with her.

Reaching the barn, Billie grabbed the pitchfork he had been working with, then turned back.

Caviness had come as far as the kitchen door to chase them, but when he saw the boy with a pitchfork, he had second thoughts. He didn't have a gun. All he had was a knife. Even though this was just a boy, the kid was nearly full grown. In a fight between a knife and a pitchfork, the pitchfork would always win.

Turning to go back through the kitchen, Caviness

grabbed a couple more pork chops, then ran out the front door and headed for his horse. He managed to get mounted just as the boy came out the front door of the house.

"You son of a bitch!" the boy called. "You bastard! You killed my ma and pa!" The boy chased after him, but couldn't catch up with the horse, which easily opened the distance between them.

Caviness hadn't noticed the boy when he first came upon the house. If he had, he might have been able to surprise the boy and take care of him first. Instead, the boy had almost managed to kill him. Caviness knew that if he was going to survive this, he was going to have to be much more careful in the future.

# TEN

Carla's house was very small, consisting of only one room, which served as a bedroom, living room, kitchen, and dining room. But using curtains and flowers and a handmade quilt, she and Jennie had done what they could to make it attractive.

The pleasant aroma of fried chicken and freshly baked biscuits greeted Preacher when he arrived.

"Please, come in. Sit down and make yourself at home," Carla said. "And excuse me for a moment while I check my biscuits."

"Everything smells good," Preacher said.

"Thank you," Carla said, returning to her work.

As Preacher watched the young woman work in the kitchen, he recalled the first time he had ever seen her. She was Jennie's friend, and had been, even then. But their chance meeting had had nothing to do with Jennie.

Preacher had just arrived in St. Louis when he heard a woman's voice call out. The cry had come from LaBarge's saloon.

"No, please, don't! It was an accident!" the woman was saying in a frightened voice.

"You bitch! I'll teach you to be clumsy around me!" a harsh voice said. The expletive was followed by a smacking sound, and as Preacher looked toward the commotion, he saw a young woman who he now knew to be Carla being propelled backward through the open front door. She fell on the porch and a large, gross-looking man stomped out of the saloon toward her.

"Please," Carla had begged. "I didn't mean to spill the beer on you." She tried to get up, but as she did so, the big man hit her again, knocking her back down onto the porch. She rolled over onto her hands and knees and tried to escape him that way, but he followed after her and kicked her. She cried out in pain.

Preacher stepped up onto the porch behind the man.

"I'll learn you to spill beer on me, you worthless whore. I'll kick your ass clear into Illinois," the man growled at Carla, who was still cowering on the wooden planks of the porch.

"Sir?" Preacher said in a calm voice from just behind the man.

"What the hell do you . . . ?" the man started to ask, but he was unable to finish his question because as soon as he turned toward Preacher, the young mountain man brought the butt of his rifle up in a smashing blow to the man's face. The blow knocked out two of the man's teeth, broke his nose, and sent a stream of blood gushing down across his mouth and into his beard. If he had been ugly before, he was grotesque now. His eyes rolled up into his head and he dropped, heavily, to the porch.

Preacher chuckled.

"What is it?" Clara asked.

"I was just thinking about the first time I ever saw you," Preacher said. "You were one miserable-looking soul."

Clara laughed as well. "I reckon I was," she said. "I don't know if I ever thanked you for coming to my rescue then."

"Oh, no more'n a dozen times," Preacher said flippantly.

Clara laughed again. "Well, here is one more time," she said. "Thank you for saving me from the clutches of a horrible man like Shardeen."

"You're welcome," Preacher said.

"Oh, I think the biscuits are done."

Using her apron as a hot pad, she pulled out a pan of golden-brown biscuits and set them on the table, beside a platter of fried chicken. She had also prepared boiled potatoes and green beans for their meal.

"Oh, this looks and smells great," Preacher said.

"Back when I lived in the House of Flowers with Jennie and the girls, I would often cook for them," Carla said. "They all said I was the best cook."

"Well, if this is any indication, I'm sure you were."

"That's why I'm working at Little Man's Café now. One of these days, I'd like to own a café of my own. Oh, I know that's probably just a foolish dream, but like Jennie used to say, a person should always hang onto their dreams."

"Jennie was a wise person," Preacher said.

"She was the wisest person I ever knew, and I miss her terribly. Actually, I miss all of the girls," Carla said. "Oh, I know, they were all whores, and the town didn't think much of them. But that's because they didn't know them the way I knew them. Why, there wasn't a one of them who wouldn't do everything they could for all the others. Especially Jennie. She was like a big sister to us all."

"She started out like a big sister to me as well," Preacher said.

Carla laughed. "I don't think Jennie thought of herself as a 'big sister' to you."

Preacher laughed as well, then coughed in embarrassment.

"No, it didn't wind up that way," he said.

"Why, Preacher. I do believe you are blushing," Carla said with a laugh. "Imagine that. Me, making you be embarrassed."

"These biscuits are really quite good," Preacher said, changing the subject and taking a bite from one.

Carla chuckled again, but she didn't tease him any further. Then, after a moment of silence, she changed the mood.

"You're going after Caviness, aren't you?" she asked.

"Yes."

"I prayed that you would," she said. "Jennie deserved better than to be killed, only to have her killer just walk away without so much as a fare-thee-well."

"Oh, Caviness isn't going to get away with it," Preacher said. "I promise you that."

"Caviness isn't the only one, you know."

"Yes, I know, but if you're talking about the man named Slater, he didn't get away with it," Preacher said. "Dog saw to that."

Carla shook her head. "I'm not talking about him. I'm talking about the man that's the cause of all of this. Theodore Epson."

"Epson? Do you mean the banker?"

"Yes."

"Well, I know Epson cheated Jennie out of her house, but what do you mean that he is the cause of all of this?"

"I've got something to show you," Carla said. Going to her dresser, she took out a letter, then brought it to Preacher.

"One night after coming home, we found this letter stuck in our door," she continued. "I think you should read it."

A single candle sat on the table, its perfectly still cone of flame lighting the distance between them. Preacher held the letter in the golden bubble of light and began to read.

*To the Harlot known as Jennie*
   *I have been informed that you are attempting to make trouble for me by accusing me of stealing. I cannot, and will not, allow my good name to be besmirched by a common whore.*

*For your own safety, I advise you to say
nothing more of what went on between us.*

*T. Epson*

"You say you found this stuck in the door?"
Preacher asked, holding it up.

"Yes," Carla answered.

"Huh. Constable Billings gave me a file he had
on Jennie, everything about her. I looked it over
pretty thoroughly this afternoon, didn't see any
mention of this," he said.

"I know. Jennie didn't mention this to him."

"Why not?"

Carla sighed and shrugged her shoulders. "I
think by the time she got this letter, she had given
up on ever getting anything done. It was like everything she took to Billings just died there."

"Well, he must've at least contacted Epson, because there was a letter from him in the file,"
Preacher said. "I believe it was from Philadelphia."

"Yes, that's where he is."

"Well, if he's in Philadelphia, then that means
he had to have someone in town leave the letter for
him."

"Caviness," Clara said.

"You're sure it was Caviness?"

Clara nodded. "I'm positive. On the night Caviness jumped out of the alley after her, he told her that
she had upset a very important man, and he warned
her not to do it anymore. That could only be Epson."

Preacher drummed his fingers on the table for a

moment. "Then Caviness killing her didn't have anything to do with me and with what happened back in Rendezvous."

"No," Carla said.

Preacher was silent for a moment. "I'm glad," he said. "That doesn't sound right," he added. "I'm not glad Epson had her killed, you understand. I'm just glad that I wasn't the reason Caviness killed her."

"Oh, Preacher, how could you ever think such a thing?" Carla asked, getting up from the table and walking over to lay her hand on his shoulder. "Why, that's as foolish as Dog thinking he was responsible."

Preacher nodded. "I know," he said. "But it was a feeling I couldn't shake until now."

"Well, I know how you feel. I've been thinking that, if I had gone with her the night she went to Mrs. Abernathy's, she wouldn't have had to come home by herself."

"She didn't have to come home by herself," Preacher replied. "She had Dog with her. And if you had been with her, you both would have been killed."

"I know, I think about that as well. Still, I just wonder if my being with her might not have made a difference."

"Do you have any idea where Caviness might be?" Preacher asked.

Carla shook her head, then returned to her chair on the opposite side of the table. "Nobody seems to know," she said." He hasn't been seen around in quite a while. In fact, he hasn't been seen since the night of the murder. That's one of the reasons everyone is so sure he is the one who did it."

They had been eating all during their conversation, and finally Preacher pushed his plate away.

"Carla, I have to tell you, that was the best meal I've eaten in years," he said.

"Well, I certainly hope you saved room for some of my apple pie," Carla said, smiling sweetly. "I baked it just for you," she added.

"Oh, apple pie? I wish you had told me earlier you were going to have apple pie. I would have for sure saved room for it," he said, rubbing his stomach.

"That's all right," Carla replied with a sweet smile. "We can always eat it after."

"After?" Preacher replied, a puzzled expression on his face.

Carla looked at Preacher with an expression of wonder and barely suppressed excitement. The pupils of her eyes grew large, and she licked her lips. Preacher had always thought she was a pretty girl, but now, at this moment, she was beautiful to him.

"After," she said again rather cryptically.

The momentary confusion rolled away. Preacher knew exactly what Carla meant. Preacher pointed toward the bed, the presence of which now seemed to dominate the single room of the little house.

"Are you talking about you and me, uh, about us being together?" he asked.

"Preacher, in all this time that I have known you, I've never said anything to you about how I felt about you. I never even made the slightest suggestion as to how I felt because . . . well, I know that you belonged to Jennie, so . . . "

"Carla, do you know what you are saying? What you are doing?" Preacher asked.

"Yes, I know exactly what I'm saying and what I'm doing," Carla said. "I'm a virgin, Preacher. All the time I was working in the house with Jennie and the other girls, Jennie insisted that I keep myself a virgin. She said that someday someone special would come along. She wanted me to wait until that some day."

Preacher sighed. "Carla, you understand that the reason nothing ever came of my relationship with Jennie is because nothing could come of it? I don't live the kind of life that would allow for a family."

"Yes, I know," Carla said.

"The same would go with us. I can't offer you anything, or promise you anything."

"I know that as well," Carla said.

"What I'm saying is that, under the circumstances, I may not be that someone special Jennie wanted you to save yourself for."

"Oh, you are the someone special, all right," Carla said.

"You are sure about this?" Preacher asked.

"I've never been more sure about anything in my life," Carla replied.

She began unbuttoning the top of her dress, but just before she opened it, she leaned forward and blew out the candle. A moment later, Preacher felt her arms around his neck, her breath on his cheek, and her soft, naked flesh against his chest.

# ELEVEN

The smell of bacon frying in the pan, and freshly brewed coffee, awakened Preacher the next morning. For just a moment, he wondered where he was. Then he remembered that he had spent the night with Carla.

He smiled as he recalled that it had been an active night.

Dog shook himself, making his loose skin flutter as he did so.

"What are you trying to tell me, Dog? That Preacher is awake?" Carla asked.

Dog walked over to the bed and lifted his paw.

"You didn't have to fix breakfast," Preacher said.

"I know I didn't have to. I wanted to," Carla said.

Preacher looked around the room.

"The necessary is out back," Carla said. "And there's a pump and washbasin just outside the back door."

"Thanks."

Preacher took care of his morning business, washed his face and hands, decided against a

shave for now, and came back into the small
house. Carla had breakfast laid out on the table.

"Carla, really . . . " he began, but Carla held up
her hand to stop him in mid-sentence.

"Preacher, this may be the closest thing to a normal
family that I'll ever have," she said. "Please, don't
deny me this pleasure."

"Deny it?" Preacher smiled broadly. "On the
contrary. I intend to enjoy every bite of it."


"Slater? Yeah, I knew him," LaBarge said, replying
to Preacher's question. "Worthless as tits on a boar
hog, that one was."

"Were he and Caviness pards?" Preacher asked.

"You goin' to buy more beer, or just ask questions?" LaBarge asked.

"I'll take another beer."

LaBarge drew a mug of beer from the barrel, then
set it in front of Preacher. Preacher blew the head off,
then took a drink.

"I wouldn't go so far as to say they was pards,"
LaBarge said. "But I did see them together from
time to time. Sometimes they'd sit at that far table
over there and talk real quiet about things."

"Things? What sort of things?"

"I don't have any idea. Like I told you, they would
talk just real quiet."

"I heard 'em palaverin' about Philadelphia
one night not too long ago," one of the other
bar patrons said. He had been standing at the
bar, about ten feet away from Preacher and

LaBarge. Supposedly, he was minding his own business, but the fact that he could respond indicated that he was paying attention to what was going on.

"What were they saying about Philadelphia?" Preacher asked.

The patron shook his head, then raised his glass for a drink. "Well, now, I can't answer that," he said. "I just heard 'em mention Philadelphia."

"Do you know some of the other folks who were at that table?"

The patron stroked his chin for a long moment, supposedly in thought, but obviously waiting for Preacher to make an offer to pay him for information. Preacher slid a nickel down the bar.

"Finch was one of them," the patron said. "They was two more. But it'll cost you a nickel a name."

"No, it won't," Preacher said.

"What do you mean it won't? I'm the one knows who was at that table."

Preacher shook his head. "Finch knows."

Finch was working at the wagon freight yard when Preacher found him. Sitting on an overturned barrel, he was packing grease into the wheel of one of the wagons.

"Your name Finch?"

Finch grabbed a handful of grease and started shoving it into the wheel hub.

"Who wants to know?"

"I do," Preacher said without identifying himself.

"I owe you money, mister?"

"No."

"Have I got your sister, wife, or daughter in a family way?"

"No."

"Did I challenge you to a duel when I was so drunk I wasn't makin' any sense?"

"No," Preacher said. He laughed.

Smiling, the wagon mechanic stood up, then extended his grease-filled hand toward Preacher's.

"Well, then, if you ain't a 'wantin' me for none of them things, I reckon I'm the man you're lookin' for."

Preacher started to take Finch's hand, but seeing it all filled with grease, he jerked his hand back.

"I'm sorry," Finch said, reacting to Preacher's aversion. "When you work in grease all the time, sometimes you just forget." He wiped his hand on his own trousers, then stuck it out for a second time. It was nearly as greasy and dirty as it had been the first time, but Preacher took it anyway.

"Now that you know who I am, what can I do for you?" Finch asked.

"Do you know Ben Caviness?"

"Caviness?" Finch's eyes narrowed. "Yes, I know the son of a bitch. Don't tell me he is a friend of yours."

Preacher shook his head.

"He's no friend of mine," he said. "But I am trying to find him. When is the last time you saw him?"

"Oh, mercy, let me see. I'd make it two or three months now, for sure."

"Have you seen him since March?"

Finch thought for a moment, then shook his head. "You mean since he killed that girl? No, and I don't reckon anyone else has either."

Preacher's eyes narrowed. "You think Caviness is the one who killed Jennie?"

"Well, folks is saying he's the one that done it, and knowin' the son of a bitch like I did, there ain't nothin' that would make me disagree with 'em."

"What about this man Slater? I hear he and Caviness were pards?"

Finch shook his head. "Well, if either one of them was goin' to have a pard, it would have to be each other," he said. "Warn't neither one of them worth a pail of warm piss. But no, I wouldn't go so far as to say that they was pards or anything like that."

"But last March, you and some others were seen sitting at the same table as both Caviness and Slater."

"Sittin' at the same table?" Finch shook his head. "No, you got me wrong, mister. I wouldn't never sit down to dinner with either one of them sorry sons of bitches."

"No, not a dinner table. A table over in LaBarge's Tavern."

"Oh. Yeah, well, I suppose I could have done that from time to time. LaBarge's gets awful crowded sometimes, so's that you can't always be none too particular who it is you wind up sittin' with."

"Do you recall sitting at a table with both Caviness

and Slater? According to one person I spoke to, they were discussing Philadelphia."

Finch tried to snap his fingers, but because of the grease, he didn't get a pop.

"I'll be damned," he said. "You know, now that you mention it, I do mind that night. Oh, LaBarge's was crowded somethin' awful that night."

"What did they say about Philadelphia, do you remember?"

"Well, it's not so much what he said, it's just that Toomey brought him a letter, and he's the one that passed the remark."

"What remark?"

"Somethin' 'bout this gettin' to be a habit, him deliverin' letters from Philadelphia."

"What did he mean by that? It being a habit?"

"According to Toomey, that was the second letter that month that come from Philadelphia."

"Thanks, Mr. Finch," Preacher said, extending his hand again.

"Wait a minute, you're the fella they call Preacher, ain't you?" Finch said as he shook Preacher's hand a second time.

"I am."

"This girl that Caviness killed, some says as how she was your woman."

"She was," Preacher said without going into any further explanation.

"I see now why you're so all-fired interested in Caviness. You aim to find 'im and kill 'im, don't you?"

"I aim to do just that,' Preacher said.

"Well, by damn, I wish you luck," Finch said.

"Anyone in this world that deserves to die, it's that son of a bitch."

"Thanks again," Preacher said.


Edgar Toomey looked up from behind the counter that separated the post office area from the customer area.

"Yes, sir?" Toomey said. "What can I do for you?"

"Sometime ago you delivered two letters to Ben Caviness. Both were from Philadelphia. Do you recall that?"

Toomey shook his head. "I'm not at liberty to discuss the U.S. mail. That's confidential information."

"Hell, what's so confidential about it?" Preacher asked. "Everyone in LaBarge's Tavern saw you deliver the letters."

"Well, if you have their word on it, why do you need confirmation from me?"

"I don't need confirmation. I know you delivered the letters. All I want to know is who sent them."

Again Toomey shook his head. "Now, you are really asking me to violate postal regulations," he said.

"You know that Caviness killed Jennie, don't you?" Preacher asked.

Toomey nodded. "I've heard that possibility discussed," he said.

"You know that, but you won't help me find him?"

"I told you, I can't answer your questions. Perhaps you should enquire over at River Bank."

Preacher looked confused. "The bank? What does that have to do with it?"

"They might be able to answer your question," Toomey said pointedly. "That's all I can do for you, do you understand? All I can do is refer you to the bank."

"I'm not sure it is appropriate for me to be discussing bank business with you," Abernathy said in response to Preacher's question.

"I don't know that we are discussing bank business," Preacher replied. "All I'm trying to do is find Ben Caviness and when I asked Mr. Toomey about it, he referred me to the bank."

"Yes, well, I . . . "

"Tell him what he wants to know, Duane," a woman's voice said.

Preacher turned to look toward the door of Abernathy's office, and saw a rather stout, stern-faced woman standing there.

"Sybil, are you . . . "

"Tell the man what he wants to know," Sybil Abernathy repeated. Her voice softened. "Please, Duane," she said. "I feel responsible for this whole awful mess. If I had not been so insistent that that beautiful young woman be run out of her house, none of this would have happened."

"What do you have to tell me?" Preacher asked Mr. Abernathy.

"Sybil, discussing the business of our depositors is highly unethical."

"So is paying someone to murder," Sybil said. "Tell him."

Mr. Abernathy sighed, then looked up at Preacher. "Caviness cashed two bank drafts, drawn against the account of Theodore Epson, on the Trust Bank of Philadelphia," he said. "The first was for fifteen dollars, and the second was for one hundred dollars."

"One hundred dollars? That's a lot of money, isn't it?"

"Yes," Abernathy agreed. "For someone like Ben Caviness, it is quite a substantial sum."

"Yes, well, I guess murder isn't cheap," Preacher said.

Once more, Constable Billings was peeling an apple. Two previously peeled and browning apples sat on the windowsill, evidence of earlier efforts.

"I think I know where Caviness is," Preacher said.

"Oh?" Billings was toward the end now, and what was clearly the longest unbroken peel he had yet made lay in a coil below the apple. He was being very careful as he continued to peel. "Where?"

"Philadelphia."

Billings looked up in surprise. "What makes you think he is in Philadelphia?"

"Because Theodore Epson is in Philadelphia."

"Epson? The man who used to be the head teller at the bank?"

"Yes. Did you know that Epson sent Caviness two bank drafts, one for fifteen dollars and one for one hundred dollars?"

"No, I didn't. What the Sam Hill would he be sending Caviness money for?"

"I think he paid Caviness to kill Jennie," Preacher replied. "If the killing had gone smooth, Caviness would've taken the money and been on his way. But it didn't go smooth. Slater got himself killed and Caviness lost an ear. And knowing Caviness, he's going to figure that he's got more money coming."

Billings nodded. "You may have an idea there," he said.

# TWELVE

Carla and Dog came down to LaClede's Landing to see Preacher off on his quest. The boat he would be taking was a side-wheeler called the *Cincinnati Queen*. Because it was designed for use on the Mississippi and Ohio, both rivers deeper and more stable than the Missouri, the *Cincinnati Queen* was larger and more ornate than the *Missouri Belle*.

There was a great deal of activity around the landing as both people and cargo were being taken aboard the three-decker, red-and-gold painted boat. William Ashley and Constable Billings had come down to the riverfront as well, and all were gathered in a little cluster as Preacher prepared to board.

"I've written a letter appointing you as my deputy," Constable Billings said, handing the letter to Preacher. "To be truthful with you, I don't know how much authority it will have, but if you find a sympathetic peace officer or judge, he might recognize it and grant some reciprocity. Sometimes law officers do that for one another, since our jurisdiction is so limited."

"Thanks," Preacher said, taking the proffered letter.

"And I've prepared several bank drafts for you which should be recognized wherever you go," Ashley said. "You have fifteen hundred dollars in fifty-dollar drafts."

"I appreciate that," Preacher said. He looked at Carla, who so far had been very quiet. Dog was sitting by Carla's side.

"Preacher, you will be careful, won't you?" Carla said. "I'm not over losin' Jennie yet. It would be awful hard on me to lose another friend just now."

"I'll be careful," Preacher promised. He looked at Dog. "Dog, you did a really good job of looking after Jennie. Now, I want you to look after Carla for me. Will you do that?"

Dog looked up at Carla, then back at Preacher. Preacher smiled, and rubbed him behind the ears. "I knew I could count on you," he said. "And I promise you this. When I return, I'll take you back to the mountains with me."

The dog opened its mouth and let its tongue hang out. Laughing, Preacher rubbed him behind his ears.

"Yeah," he said. "I thought you would like that."

The boat's whistle blew and, looking toward the boat, they saw the purser coming up to the bow, which was pegged against the bank. The purser raised a megaphone.

"All aboard that's comin' aboard!" he shouted.

There were several last-minute good-byes as those

who had remained ashore, including Preacher, started up the gangplank.

"Stand clear!" one of the deckhands shouted as he closed the gate.

"Stand by to cast off!" the captain shouted down from the wheelhouse.

"Standing by!" the deckhand answered.

"Cast off."

The deckhand lifted the heavy rope from its stanchion and threw it toward the bank. The boat's whistle blew two deep-throated blasts that echoed from the opposite side of the river. The engine was put in reverse and the steam boomed out of the steam-relief pipe like the firing of a cannon. Like the boat whistle, the booming came back in echo from the Illinois side of the river.

The wheel began spinning backward, and the boat pulled away from the dock, then turned with the wheel going upriver and the bow pointed downstream. The engine lever was slipped to full forward, and the wheel began spinning in the other direction until it caught hold to begin propelling the boat downstream.

Walking back to the stern of the boat, Preacher looked toward the landing they had just departed and saw that though many had left, Carla and Dog were still standing there, watching as the boat moved quickly downriver. Preacher stood there looking back at them until the boat moved around a bend in the river, taking them out of sight.

\*\*\*

The Mississippi River was placid, though with a current powerful enough to push the steamboat south at a fairly good clip. It was nearly dusk and the sun, low in the west, caused the river to shimmer in a pale blue, with highlights of reflected gold.

As Preacher stood on the deck, he recalled his first experience on the river. As a twelve year-old boy looking for adventure, he had met a man named Pete Harding at a trading post on the Ohio River. Harding was taking a flatboat down the Ohio. The boat was loaded with goods to be traded at the Mississippi River port town of New Madrid, and Harding hired Art as his deckhand and assistant. It was a position young Art accepted readily, for not only was it a job, it provided him with food and transportation for his trek westward.

*Fifteen years earlier*

"Run away from home, did you, boy?" Harding asked.

"No, I . . ." the boy started to reply, but deciding it would be better to be honest with Harding, he sighed and spoke the truth. "Yes, sir, I ran away from home."

"Having trouble there, were you?"

"No, sir, I wasn't havin' any trouble. It's just that I wanted to . . . ." He let the sentence trail off.

"You wanted to see the creature."

"See the creature?"

"That's a saying, son, for folks like you and me."

"You and me?"

"It would be my guess that you and I are just alike," Harding said. "There are some folks who are born, live, and die and never get more'n ten miles away from home in any direction. Then there's those folks, like the two of us, that's always wondering what's on the other side of the next hill. And when they get over that hill, why, damn me if they don't feel like they got to go on to the next one, and the next one, and the next one after that. They're always hopin' they'll find somethin' out there, some sort of creature they ain't never seen before. I know it's that way with me, and I'm reckonin' that it's the same way with you."

The boy laughed. He had never heard it put that way before, but he knew that Harding had pegged it exactly as it was.

"Yes, sir," he said. "That's the way it is with me. I want to see the creature."

The boy went to New Madrid with Harding, but there, one night, he was hit over the head.

Art felt the sun warming his face, but that was the only thing about him that felt good. He had a tremendous headache, and he was very nauseous. He was lying down. Even though he had not yet opened his eyes, he knew he was lying on sun-dried wood, because he could smell it. He was also in motion. He could feel that, and he heard the creak and groan of turning wagon wheels and the steady clopping sound of hooves.

The last thing he remembered was leaving the tavern to go to the privy. What was he doing here? For that matter, where exactly *was* here?

Art opened his eyes. It was a mistake. The sun was glaring, and the moment he opened his eyes, two bolts of pain shot through him.

"He's awake," a girl's voice said.

Putting his hand over his eyes, Art opened them again. Now that he was shielding his eyes from the intense sunlight, it wasn't as painful to open them. Peering through the separations between his fingers, he looked at the girl who had spoken. She appeared to be about his age, with long dark curls and vivid amber eyes staring intently at him.

"Who are you?" Art asked.

"My name is Jennie," she replied.

That was Preacher's introduction to the girl, later to become a woman who would be so important to him.

Preacher soon learned that Jennie was actually a slave girl belonging to Lucas Younger, the man who owned the wagon in which he was riding. To his surprise, he discovered that he was being considered a slave as well. Because he had no proof of his identity, the mere suggestion that he was a slave was enough to make Younger's claim credible.

The boy escaped, spent time with the Indians, then found his way to St. Louis, where he worked in a wagon freight yard. Then, two years later, when General Jackson raised an army of volunteers from the Mississippi and Ohio River valleys to go to New Orleans to fight against the British, the boy was reunited with Pete Harding.

Pete Harding was killed in the Battle of New Orleans. Preacher was mustered out of the Army after the battle, and even though he was but fourteen, he was discharged as a lieutenant. And in keeping with his promise to Pete Harding, Preacher went west to the Rocky Mountains to "see the creature."

After a full day's run from St. Louis, the *Cincinnati Queen* put in at Cape Girardeau, Missouri. There, merchants from the town came on board the boat to sell their goods. This was the ultimate destination for many of the passengers, who disembarked, while others left the boat merely for a stroll around town. In the meantime, the boat took on a fresh supply of wood for its continuing journey.

From Cape Girardeau, the boat continued south on the river until it reached the confluence of the Mississippi and Ohio Rivers. There, the *Cincinnati Queen* turned up the Ohio. Leaving Missouri behind, it journeyed north and east, bordered on the south by the state of Kentucky, and on the north by the fertile farming fields of Illinois.

After it entered the Ohio River, forward progress became much, much slower because it was now necessary for the boat to beat its way against the current. However, proceeding at a pace that was only slightly faster than a man could walk, the boat continued on its journey.

Without even realizing it, Preacher was growing more and more tense until, five days after they turned up the Ohio, he realized what had been making him so tense. He was about to come face-to-face with his past. Standing at the rail, he watched the shore slide by slowly, monotonously, almost hypnotically. And, as vividly as if he were reliving it, he remembered the past.

*Fifteen years earlier*

Leaving his brother sleeping in the bed behind him, the boy who would one day be called Preacher stepped out of the bedroom into the upstairs hallway. He moved to the end of the hall to his parents' bedroom, where he stood just outside their door for a moment, listening to his pa's heavy snoring.

His pa's snores were loud because he slept hard. He worked hard too, eking out a living for his family by laboring from dawn to dusk on a farm that was more rock than dirt, and took more than it gave.

His ma was in there too, though her rhythmic breathing could scarcely be heard over her husband's snores. She was always the last to go to bed and the first to get up. It was nearly two hours before dawn now, but Art, the boy who would one day be called Preacher, knew that his mother would be rolling out of bed in less than an hour, starting another of the endless procession of backbreaking days that were the borders of her life.

"Ma, Pa, I want you both to know that I ain't

leavin' 'cause of nothin' either of you have done," the boy said quietly. "You have been good to me, and there ain't no way I can ever pay you back for all that you have done for me, or let you know how much I love you. But the truth is, I got me a hankerin' to get on with my life, and I reckon twelve years is long enough to wait."

From there, the boy moved down to his sisters' room. He went into their room and saw them sleeping together in the bed his father had made for them. A silver splash of moonlight fell through the window, illuminating their faces. One was sucking her thumb, a habit she practiced even in her sleep; the other was clutching a corncob doll. The sheet had slipped down, so Preacher pulled it back up, covering their shoulders. The two girls, eight and nine, snuggled down into the sheets, but didn't awaken.

"I reckon I'm going to miss seeing you two girls grow up," the boy said quietly. "But I'll always keep you in my mind, along with Ma, Pa, and my brother."

His good-byes having been said, Preacher picked up the pillowcase in which he had put a second shirt, another pair of pants, three biscuits, and an apple, and started toward the head of the stairs.

Although he had been planning this adventure for a couple of months, he hadn't made the decision to actually leave until three days ago. On that day he'd stood on a bluff and watched a flatboat drift down the Ohio River, which flowed passed the family farm. There was a family on the flatboat, holding on tightly to the little pile of canvas-covered goods that represented all their worldly possessions. One of the boat's passengers, a boy about Preacher's age, waved. Other than the wave, there had been nothing unusual about that particular boat. It was one of many similar vessels that passed by the farm every week.

To anyone else, seeing an entire family uprooted and looking for a new place to live, traveling the river with only those possessions they could carry on the boat with them, might have been a pitiful sight. But to a young boy with wanderlust, it was an adventure that stirred his soul, and he wished more than anything that he could be with them.

On the morning Art left, he was nearly to the bottom of the stairs when the sudden chiming of the Eli Terry clock startled him. Gasping, he nearly dropped his sack, but recovered in time. He smiled sheepishly at his reaction. The beautifully decorated clock, which sat on the mantel over the fireplace, was the family's most prized possession. His mother once told him with great pride that someday the clock would be his. He reckoned now that it would go to his brother. His brother always put more store in the clock than he did anyway.

Recovering his poise, he took a piece of paper from his pocket, and put it on the mantel beside the clock. It was addressed to "Ma and Pa."

At first he hadn't planned to tell anyone in his family that he was leaving. He was just going to go, and when his folks woke up for the next day's chores they would find him gone. But at the last minute, he'd thought his parents might rest a little easier if they knew he had left on his own, and had not been stolen in the middle of the night.

The boy had enough schooling to enable him to read and write a little. He wasn't that good at it, but he was good enough to leave a note.

*Ma and Pa*
   *Don't look for me, for I have went away. I am near a man now and I want to be on my own. Love, your son, Arthur.*

With the note in place, Arthur opened the front door quietly and stepped out onto the porch. It was still dark outside, and the farm was a cacophony of sound: frogs on the pond, singing insects clinging to the tall grass, and the whisper of the night wind through a nearby stand of elm trees.

Once he was out of the house and off the porch, the boy moved quickly down the path that led to the river. When he reached the bluff, he turned and looked back. The house loomed large in the moonlight, a huge dark slab against the dull gray of the night. The window to his parents' bedroom was gleaming softly in the moonlight. It looked like a tear-glistened eye, a symbol that wasn't lost on him. A lump came to his throat, his eyes stung, and for a moment, he actually considered abandoning his departure plans. But then he squared his shoulders.

"No," he said aloud. "I ain't goin' to stand here and cry like a baby. I said I'm a'goin', and by damn I'm goin'." He turned away from the house.

"Sorry about sayin' 'damn,' Ma, but I reckon if

I'm goin' to be a man, I'm goin' to have to start talkin' like a man."

The boy left the beaten path, then picked his way through the brush down to the side of the river's edge. To the casual observer, there was nothing there, but when he started pulling branches aside, he uncovered a small skiff.

He had found the boat earlier in the year during the spring runoff. No doubt it had broken from its moorings somewhere when the river was at its freshet stage, though it was impossible to ascertain where it had come from. He hadn't actually stolen the boat, but he did hide it, even from his father. And he assured himself that if someone had come looking for the boat, he would have disclosed its location. But as no search materialized, at least none of which he was aware, he got to keep the boat.

The boat provided him with a golden opportunity, and it wasn't until it came into his possession that he seriously began considering running away from home. He left, not because of any abuse, but because of pure wanderlust.

# THIRTEEN

*Portsmouth, Ohio*

Preacher thought about it before he left the *Cincinnati Queen*. Should he or should he not visit his family? If he did visit them, how would they react? Would they welcome him, or would they resent him? If they reacted with resentment, it would certainly be an emotion he could understand. In all the time he had been gone, he had never once contacted them, to let them know whether he was dead or alive.

Dead or alive.

He suddenly realized that he didn't know whether or not his parents, or indeed any of his family, were dead or alive. The thought gave him pause, especially because he realized that, until this very moment, it wasn't anything he had ever considered before.

Was it confidence that they were alive that kept the worry from his mind? Or was it extreme self-ishness on his part?

He didn't want to face up to that shortcoming in his own personality, but if truth be told, he would have to say that it was because of his own extreme selfishness.

That consideration made up his mind for him. When the boat reached the point nearest the old family homestead, he would get off and seek them out. He could only hope that they were all still alive, and were still in the same place. Further, he could only hope that they would accept him.

He did not feel that he was compromising his mission by leaving the boat to search for them. After all, there was no sense of immediacy to what he was doing. Jennie was dead, and would remain dead. There was only a need to bring about justice, and that he would do.

Portsmouth, Ohio, was the nearest town to the old homestead. As it turned out, it was also a scheduled stop for the boat, though primarily because it was a place to replenish the wood supply.

As the boat pulled ashore, Preacher visited the purser's office and informed him that he would like to get off there.

"But you've purchased a ticket all the way to Steubenville," the purser replied. "We are quite a long ways from Steubenville."

"Yes, I know, but I would like to visit Portsmouth."

The purser chuckled. "I've seen Portsmouth, mister. Believe me, it isn't much to look at."

"Maybe so. But I'm getting off here."

"All right. Will you want to be going on to Steubenville at a later time?"

"Yes. Can I buy another ticket from here?"

"Well, if you are going through, that won't be

necessary," the purser said. "You've already bought the ticket." The purser handed Preacher a little slip of paper. "Just present this to the purser of the next boat belonging to the Ohio and Mississippi Line that stops here, and he will honor it for passage on to Steubenville."

"Thanks," Preacher said, folding the paper and putting it in his pocket.

Several toots of the boat's whistle indicated that it was about to dock. That was followed by the slight jolt of the bow as the captain pegged it on the shore.

"Make fast the lines!" the captain called down, and at the bow, the deckhands secured the boat to the shore.

Preacher waited until the gangplank was stretched down from the side. Then he left the boat, climbed up the cobblestone-covered riverbank, and stood there for a moment, looking out over the town of his youth. As he stood there looking at the town, the town was looking back at him, or at least, several of the town's citizens. He was not their typical visitor.

Preacher had not brought his rifle with him, deciding to leave it for safekeeping with his friend William Ashley back in St. Louis. But he had brought his knife and his pistol, and he was wearing both of them on a belt that he had strapped around his waist. His clothes consisted of a buckskin shirt and trousers, as well as a rather wide-brimmed hat.

Preacher wandered through the town, looking it over carefully. Oddly, it was a little like trying to recall a dream that slips away so quickly after waking, for while he recognized some of the buildings, many he did not.

One of the buildings that he did recognize was the Riverman's Inn, on the corner of Third and Court Streets. He remembered it, even though he had never been inside the building. That was because the Riverman's Inn was a saloon, and as Preacher had been so young when he left Portsmouth, this saloon wasn't a place he had ever visited. Preacher paused just in front, his hand resting on the door frame for a moment before he went inside.

Although this was the first time he had ever been inside the establishment, there was a degree of familiarity about it. Like most of the saloons and taverns he had been in, this one had a bar that ran down one side of the room. The bar had a foot rail, as well as rings every ten feet or so, from which hung towels for the customers' use. In addition to the bar, there was a handful of tables out on the floor.

All of the tables were empty. In fact, the bar was empty as well. There were only two people in the place, a man behind the bar and an attractive young woman who was standing at the far end of the bar. For a moment Preacher felt there was something different about the young woman. Then he realized what it was. She wasn't dressed in the provocative style that he had come to associate with bar girls. Preacher didn't know if that was unique to this particular woman, or if all bar women back East dressed in a more conservative fashion.

Both the man and the woman looked toward him as he came inside.

"Good afternoon, sir," the man said to Preacher, greeting him with a friendly smile. "Welcome to the Riverman's Inn. You just get off the boat, did you?"

"I did," Preacher said.

"I thought so." He tapped his finger to his temple. "I have the power of divination, you know."

The woman laughed. "Don't let Vaughan fool you, mister. It's your clothes that give you away. Nobody around here wears that kind of clothes. What do you call that?"

"Buckskins," Preacher replied. "They are useful in my line of work."

"And what would that line of work be?" the bartender asked.

"I'm a fur trapper."

"A fur trapper, is it?" the man replied. "Well, now, that sounds fascinating. Have a drink, sir. The first one is on the house," the bartender said as he drew the beer.

"And if I don't order a second?" Preacher replied.

The man laughed. "Well, then, the first one is still on the house and I'm the fool for thinking it would generate more business for me."

Preacher laughed as well. "You're no fool, mister. That seems to me like a friendly way to welcome new customers."

"Doesn't hurt to be friendly, and I can afford to give away a drink now and then," the man said. He put the beer mug in front of Preacher. "There you go, sir."

"Thanks," Preacher said. Picking up the mug, he blew the foam off the mug, then took a long swallow.

"A fur trapper, you say?"

"Yes."

"You know, I think folks used to trap some around here years ago. But most of the trapping now is out West somewhere. And from the looks of you, I'd say that's where you would be doing your trapping—out West somewhere."

"Yes," Preacher said. "I trap in the Rocky Mountains."

"I've never seen the Rocky Mountains, but I would truly like to. I've heard they are something awesome to behold."

"They are indeed," Preacher said. He finished the beer. "Now, I wonder if you would let me buy one for each of you."

"Well, sir, that's kind of you to offer," the bartender said. "But if all I did was stay here all day drinking my own product, I'd be too drunk to work."

"And the lady?"

"The lady is my wife," the bartender said. "And she don't drink at all. Can you imagine, marryin' a tavern keeper and not even drinkin'?"

"Yes, if she's drawn to the man and not what he does," Preacher said. "I'll have another for myself then."

The bartender drew a second drink.

"Well, here's to you both," Preacher said, paying for a second drink, then holding it up to them.

"What brings you from a place as glorious as the Rocky Mountains to a tiny place like Portsmouth?" the bartender asked.

"I'm just traveling through," Preacher said. "Heading for Philadelphia."

"Philadelphia," the bartender said. "Have you ever been there?"

"No, I haven't."

"I think you will find it a fascinating place to visit. I was there a year or so back myself."

The woman laughed. "It was more like ten years," she said. "We wasn't even married yet when you went."

"The name is Vaughan Roberts," the bartender said, sticking his hand out by way of introduction. "And whatever it is that caused you to stop by our fair town, you are truly welcome."

"Thanks," Preacher said. "Folks call me Preacher."

"Preacher? And would you be a man of the cloth, Preacher?"

Preacher chuckled. "Far from it, I'm afraid. It just seems to be a name I've picked up."

"Ever been here before, Preacher?" Vaughan asked.

"Yes," Preacher said. "As a matter of fact, I am from here. I used to live here, or not far from here, when I was a boy."

"You don't say? So that explains why you dropped by. You wanted to visit the place of your youth."

"You might say that," Preacher agreed. "I lived upriver a few miles. My folks had a place there, just where the river makes a big sweep."

"Well, there's a couple of places up there," Vaughan said. "But that's pretty good land. Finest land in the country, some folks say. What is it that made your family up and leave like they done?"

"Oh, you misunderstood me. My family didn't leave at all," Preacher said. "They are still here. Or at least, as far as I know, they are still here."

"As far as you know? Here, that's a mighty strange thing to say about your own family. You mean you don't even know if they are still here?"

"I'm ashamed to say that I don't know," Preacher said. He took another drink before he continued. "You see, I told you I left here when I was a boy, and that's just what I did. As I look back on it now, I probably did a bad thing, but when I was twelve years old, I just up and left on my own."

Suddenly the woman gasped, and put her hand to her mouth. "Oh, my," she said in a soft voice. "Oh, my, oh, my, oh, my."

"Tess, what in the world has got into you?" Vaughan asked.

"Tess?" Preacher repeated in a quiet voice. He looked at the young woman. "Is that your name? Tess?"

Tears sprang into Tess's eyes, and she nodded. "Yes," she answered.

"Would you have a sister named Betty, and a brother named Morgan?"

"I also have a brother named Arthur," Tess

replied, now smiling broadly through her tears. "We thought he was lost, but I know now that he has come back to us."

"My God," Vaughan said, now realizing what was going on. He stared at Preacher. "You are Arthur, aren't you? You are Tess's long-lost brother."

"I reckon I am," Preacher said.

With a little cry, Tess ran into Art's arms. He embraced her for a long moment, feeling her against him, feeling her tears wet his cheeks.

Finally, Tess drew away from him. "Why?" she asked. It was more of a sob than a question. "Oh, Arthur, why in heaven's name did you run away from us like that?"

"I'm sorry, Tess," Preacher said. It was the only way he could think of to respond to this question that had no answer. "I'm sorry."

Vaughan closed his place for the rest of the day, hitched a team to a wagon, then drove Tess and her long-lost brother out to her parents' farm.

"I've got a thousand questions I want to ask you," Tess said as they drove along the dirt road that ran parallel with the river. "But I'm going to save them because I know that everyone else will want to ask the same questions, and there's no sense in making you say everything twice."

"Thanks," Preacher said. "I'll answer all the questions as best I can, I promise."

Tess's promise not to ask a lot of questions caused the ride out to be a quiet one, and Preacher welcomed the silence because it gave him time to reconnect with his past. As the wagon rolled along the road, Preacher looked out over the landscape, trying to reconcile what he was seeing with memories. As it was mostly trees and plowed fields, there wasn't anything significant enough to make an impression on him. That is until they came around the final bend and he saw the house, a white, two-story house, sitting on a small hill.

The house was exactly the same. The final moments before he'd left, indelibly burned into his mind and heart, were recreated by what he was seeing now. For a minute, all the intervening years between the time he stood there as a twelve-year-old boy, fighting tears, and this moment rolled away. It was as if the years of his life had formed one, long ribbon, and someone had grabbed the ribbon at each end and folded it together, connecting past with present so that it was impossible to differentiate one from the other.

The wagon pulled into the front yard, and his mother came out onto the porch.

"Well, hello, Tess, Vaughan," she said. She was holding a dish towel. "I didn't expect to see you two until this weekend. Who's your friend?"

"Mom, this is . . . ," Tess started, but she didn't finish. Suddenly, the woman on the porch gasped, and put her hand to her chest. Her eyes grew wide and her mouth began to tremble.

"Don't tell me," she said. "I know who it is." With her arms open wide, she hurried down from the porch. "Arthur," she said. "My dear, sweet, Arthur!"

"How did she recognize me after all these years?" Preacher asked quietly as he stepped down from the wagon to go toward his mother.

"Mothers have a way of knowing these things," Tess said. Even though Tess was not a mother, and was younger than Preacher, she was already in touch with the wisdom that is peculiar only to women.

At supper time, Preacher sat at the dining room table with his mother and father, Tess and Vaughan, Betty and her husband, Jim, and Morgan and his wife, Ann, and their young son, Art.

Preacher's father was holding the Bible.

"A reading from St. Luke," Preacher's father began. He looked up at everyone at the table, then, clearing his voice, began to read.

*"A certain man had two sons; and the younger of them said to his father, Father, give me the portion of goods that falleth to me. And he divided unto him his living.*

*"And not many days after, the younger son gathered all together, and took his journey into a far country, and there wasted his substance with riotous living.*

*"And when he had spent all, there arose a mighty famine in that land; and he began to be in want.*

*"And he went and joined himself to a citizen of that country; and he sent him into the field to feed swine.*

*"And he would fain have filled his belly*

*with the husks that the swine did eat; and no
man gave unto him.*

*"And when he came to himself, he said,
How many hired servants of my father's have
bread enough and to spare, and I perish with
hunger!*

*"I will arise and go to my father and will
say unto him, Father, I have sinned against
heaven and before thee, and am no more worthy to be called thy son. Make me as one of thy
hired servants.*

*"And he arose, and came to his father, but
when he was yet a great way off, his father
saw him, and had compassion, and ran and
fell on his neck, and kissed him.*

*"And the son said unto him, Father, I have
sinned against heaven, and in thy sight, and
am no more worthy to be called thy son.*

*"But the father said to his servants, Bring
forth the best robe, and put it on him; and put
a ring on his hand, and shoes on his feet. And
bring hither the fatted calf, and kill it; and let
us eat, and be merry."*

Preacher's father closed the book and looked
across the table at his son.

"And, like the father in the Bible, I welcome my
returning son. He was lost, and now he is found."

There was a moment of silence, then Morgan
spoke. "Hey, Pop, we didn't kill any fatted calves,
though. All Mom did was wring the neck of a couple
of chickens. You think that will count the same?"

Everyone at the table laughed.

Later, after dinner, Preacher's father took a couple of chairs out onto the front porch, and invited Preacher to join him. Although everyone wanted to talk to him, to hear his story and to find out where he had been and what he had done, they all acquiesced to Preacher's father, giving him his just due.

"Have you taken up smoking, son?"

"Yes."

"Suppose we light our pipes and have a talk."

"All right."

A cool breeze blew across the porch and, from there, they could hear the whisper of the Ohio River as it moved by in front of them. The sun was low, and the river was a translucent blue, gleaming as if with its own light. The two men lit their pipes, then sat there for a long, quiet moment, enveloped in the smoke of their own making.

Preacher knew that his father must have a thousand questions, so he said nothing. He waited patiently for his father to begin the conversation. He was surprised by the first thing his father said.

"It's been my experience that men who wear a gun and a knife like that generally know how to use them. Are you skilled with those weapons?"

"I get by," Preacher said.

"Ever killed anyone?"

"Only in self-defense, Pa. It's not something I take pleasure in."

"Tess said you introduced yourself in the tavern as Preacher. How'd you come by a name like that?"

Preacher told his father the story of how, as a captive of the Indians, he had preached a sermon continuouslyfor twenty-four hours, convincing the Indians that he was crazy, thus causing them to spare his life.

"Folks heard about that," he concluded, "and I've been called Preacher ever since."

Preacher's father laughed. "That's a wonderful story, son," he said. "And a fitting name. But if you don't mind, while you are here, we'll call you Arthur, the way you were born."

"I don't mind at all," Preacher replied.

"Now, tell me, if you can, why you up and left us in the middle of the night, without so much as a by your leave."

"I wanted to see the creature," Preacher said, remembering the expression used by Pete Harding.

"To see the creature," Pa repeated.

"Yes, sir."

"And did you see the creature?"

Preacher was quiet for a long moment before he answered.

"Yes, sir. I think you could say that I have seen the creature," he replied.

"Tell me about it," his father said.

Preacher began speaking then, starting the story from the morning he sneaked out of the house and onto the boat, telling about his encounter with river pirates, about being declared a slave by Lucas Younger, about his experiences in the war, and about his experiences in the mountains.

He left nothing out, including his relationship

with Jennie. He even told his father that Jennie was one-quarter black and, according to the laws of Missouri and other slave-holding states, legally considered a Negro for purposes of slavery. And he told his father that the reason he was going to Philadelphia was to find the man who killed her.

"And what do you aim to do with him when you find him?" his father asked.

"I aim to kill 'im, Pa."

His father was quiet for a moment. "Well, I don't hold with killin', but then, that's my world, not yours. I won't fault you for livin' in your world, seein' as it's the only one you've got now, and we all have to do what we have to do."

"Yes, sir, that's pretty much the way I look at it too," Preacher said.

It was now nearly one o'clock in the morning. Tess and Vaughan had left for town long ago, and the others were sound asleep. Still, Preacher and his father talked. Preacher found that it was as necessary for him to fill his father in on what had happened to him over the past several years as it was for his father to know.

Finally, stories were finished and the two men sat in silence for a long moment, listening to the sound of the night creatures.

"I read the story of the Prodigal Son for a reason," Preacher's father said, finally breaking the silence. "Not because I thought you had been a wastrel, living a life of debauchery and sin. You were a good boy when you were twelve, and I couldn't see anything, any temptation, that would change you.

"No, sir. I read the story because I wanted you to know that, despite all that's happened, I'm happy you came back. My one prayer, for all these years, has been that I could see you at least one more time, to satisfy myself that you are still alive and well."

Preacher didn't answer.

"Are you satisfied with the life you are living, boy?"

"Yes, Pa, I am," Preacher said, realizing at that moment that he was very satisfied. "I can't think of anything I would rather do than what I'm doing now."

"I'm glad. You won't mind, then, if I leave all the farm to Morgan, who has stayed here and worked it for his whole life."

"I think that would be the only right thing to do," Preacher said.

"I'm glad you feel that way, for that's what I intend to do. That is, if I'm able to hold onto it."

"Able to hold onto it? What do you mean?"

"You've told me your story," Preacher's father said. "Now, maybe it's time I told you mine."

Although neither Preacher nor his father realized it, Morgan had heard every word of their conversation. His and Ann's room was just above the front porch, and because it was a warm night, his window was open. The breeze the open window allowed in also brought to him, very clearly, the conversation his brother and father were having.

Until his father said what he did to Art, Morgan had no idea that his father was planning on leaving everything to him.

He was pleased to hear Preacher agree to his father's plan. And now, as his father explained the difficulty they were in, Morgan felt that his older brother would be able to help them. He didn't know how, but he was confident that he would.

# FOURTEEN

Klyce Blanton owned the Security Bank of Ohio. He had only recently purchased the bank, and immediately upon acquisition had let it be known that it would no longer be business as usual.

"No more mollycoddling of debtors," he said. "From now on, every penny owed to this bank must be paid on the date it is owed, or I will foreclose."

It was no coincidence that Blanton acquired the bank at the time when a severe drought had brought about crop failure for many of the farmers, Preacher's father included. Blanton bought the bank for the express purpose of forcing all the neighboring farmers into default so he could take their land at a fraction of its actual worth. He had already foreclosed on several farms.

Under the previous banker, the farmers had been able to arrange for additional time by paying the interest only when their note came due. It was a normal procedure, and Preacher's father had not the slightest idea that he would not be allowed to do so until he went to the bank to make his payment. That was when he was informed that Klyce intended to exercise his legal right to call the note the moment it was due.

"That's two weeks from now," Sylvanias said. "The land that my father cleared, and that I have nurtured all these years, the land that I intended to pass down to my children, is being taken away from me, and there is nothing I can do about it."

Preacher said nothing to his father, but at the earliest opportunity he planned to go into town and set things right. It was the least he could do after causing them so many years of worry and heartache.

Getting up early, Preacher came down the stairs and left a note on the kitchen table.

> *Dear Ma and Pa*
> *I have some business to take care of so I must be gone for a while. But don't worry, I will be back today.*
>
> *Your son, Art*

Preacher walked into Portsmouth, arriving around eight o'clock, just as the town was beginning its daily activity. Though it was much smaller than St. Louis, it had a cosmopolitan air about it with its businesses and enterprises. Merchants were in front of their establishments, industriously sweeping their porches. Freight wagons were already rolling in and out of the town, some of them queuing up at the river's edge in preparation for meeting the next arriving boat.

Preacher walked by Dunnigan's Mercantile store

and saw that Mr. Dunnigan, wearing an apron, was putting together a display of some of his goods. Preacher recognized Dunnigan right away because the merchant hadn't changed that much over the last fifteen years. Preacher smiled as he recalled that he had worked for Dunnigan one summer, sacking potatoes.

"Good morning, Mr. Dunnigan," Preacher said, touching the brim of his hat.

"Good morning, young man," Dunnigan replied cheerily. It was obvious that Dunnigan didn't recognize him, and Preacher didn't say who he was because he didn't want to have to go into a long explanation as to where he had been all these years. "Looks like it's going to be a nice day," Dunnigan added.

"Yes, sir, it does indeed," Preacher replied, continuing on toward the bank.

The bank was on Front Street. It was closed, but on the front door was a sign that said it would open for business at nine o'clock. Looking through the window of the bank, Preacher could see the clock inside. It was now eight twenty-three.

For the next few minutes, passersby saw Preacher standing in front of the bank. From all outward appearances, he seemed totally relaxed, with his arms folded across his chest and one foot raised and pressing against the front wall. In truth, he was keenly alert, both mentally and physically, for whatever challenge he might have to face.

Shortly before nine, a fancy carriage, accompanied by a rider on either side, turned onto Front Street and came toward the bank. The carriage stopped in front and the passenger climbed down.

"Will you be needing the carriage this morning, Mr. Blanton?" the driver asked.

"No," the passenger answered. The man was grossly overweight, with large jowls and several chins. He had virtually no neck, so his bald head seemed to rest, like a cannonball, on his round shoulders.

"Very good, sir. I'll be over at the livery if you do need me." The driver clucked to his team and the carriage pulled away.

The fat man looked at Preacher, curious as to who he was.

"Are you Klyce Blanton?" Preacher asked.

"I am he, sir. Why do you ask? Are you waiting for the bank to open?"

"Yes."

"Well, I'm always glad to do business," Blanton said as he unlocked the bank door. "But the bank doesn't open for another fifteen minutes."

"I'll wait," Preacher said, making no effort to move.

"What sort of business do you have with the bank?" Blanton asked.

"I'm here to give you some money," Preacher said.

Blanton smiled broadly. "Well, now, if you are here to give me money, I think we can make an exception and let you in a little early. Come on inside, Mr. . . . "

"Preacher."

"Preacher? Your name is Preacher?"

"Preacher will do."

"Well, Mr. Preacher, come on inside and we'll do some business."

The two men who had accompanied Blanton, both armed and rough-looking, tied their horses off at the hitching rail, then went inside as well. One of them sat in a chair by the front door, while the other walked toward the back office with Preacher and Blanton. This one settled in a chair just outside the door to Blanton's office.

"These two rather formidable-looking gentlemen are my bodyguards," Blanton explained when he saw Preacher looking at them. "A man of my prominence can't afford to be without protection. Now, I believe you said something about being here to give me money?"

"That's right."

"Well, then, Mr. Preacher, come on into my office and we'll take care of business. Are you opening an account with us?"

"No," Preacher said. "I'm here to pay off a loan and pick up the paper you hold on a farm."

The smile left Blanton's face and his eyes narrowed. He stroked his multiple chins as he stared at Preacher.

"What makes you think you can just come in here and buy up a loan?" he asked. He pointed to Preacher's buckskin clothes. "I can tell you aren't from around here, but that's not the way business is done."

"I'm not buying up a loan," Preacher said. "I'm paying one off. I want it returned to the borrower, free and clear."

"Why would you want to pay off someone else's loan?"

"It's the loan my pa borrowed against his farm," Preacher said. "I want him out from under that debt."

"Who is your father?"

"Sylvanias Coopersmith," Preacher said.

As Preacher said the name Coopersmith, he realized that it was the first time he had so much as spoken the name in over fifteen years. When he left home he had purposely dropped his last name in order not to bring any discredit on his family.

Blanton shook his head. "Are you trying to pull something on me, mister? I know Sylvanias Coopersmith's son, Morgan, and you aren't Morgan."

"I'm his other son, Art."

"I thought you said your name was Preacher."

"That's what folks call me, and I'm comfortable with it," Preacher replied.

"You know I think, mister? I think you are a liar," Blanton snarled.

As quickly as a striking snake, Preacher pulled his knife and stuck the point of it into Blanton's left nostril. He sliced the side of the nostril, not a very large cut, but one that went all the way through. It was not only painful, it produced a lot of blood.

"Ahhh!" Blanton shouted, grabbing his wounded nose. "Colby!"

The bodyguard who was posted just outside Blanton's office came running in through the door, his pistol in his hand. Spinning toward him, Preacher threw his knife, and the point of it punched through Colby's sleeve, pinning his gun hand to the wall just inside the door.

The other bodyguard came running in as well, but as soon as he stepped through the door he was greeted with Preacher's drawn pistol, charged, cocked, and leveled right at him. The second bodyguard stopped dead in his tracks and threw up his hands. "No, wait! Hold it, hold it!" he called out in quick fear.

"Mr. Blanton, you might want to rethink what you just said," Preacher said calmly. "You see, where I'm from, a man's word is his bond. When you call someone a liar, you commit a serious offense against his person."

Blanton held his hand cupped under his nose and the palm was pooling with blood.

"What?" Blanton replied, his voice strained with pain and distraction.

"Whenever someone calls me a liar, I take it real personal," Preacher said.

"I . . . I didn't mean that I actually thought you were a liar. I just didn't realize that Mr. Coopersmith had a son other than Morgan," Blanton whined.

"I thought that might be the case," Preacher said. He looked at the two bodyguards, who were glaring at him with anger. "You," he said to Colby.

"Bring my knife to me. And be careful how you do it."

Still glaring, Colby pulled the knife from his sleeve and the wall, then brought it back to Preacher, handing it to him handle-first.

"Thank you. Now, I'd like for both of you to put your pistols on Mr. Blanton's desk," Preacher said, motioning with his own pistol.

Still glaring at him, the men started across the room with their pistols.

"Uh,-uh," Preacher said. "Carry them by their barrels."

Both pistols were cocked, and the men stopped, then started to ease the hammers down.

"No, I want you to leave your guns cocked," Preacher said.

"Are you crazy? You expect me to hold a cocked pistol by the barrel?" Colby asked.

Preacher smiled coldly. "Yes, I do," he said. "That way I know you will be careful."

Slowly, gingerly, the two bodyguards turned the pistols around and held them by the barrel. As Preacher had ordered, the pistols were still cocked. Then, carefully, the men walked the rest of the way across the floor and put the pistols on the desk.

"Thank you. Now, if you would, I want both of you to go over there and sit on the floor facing the wall."

"Mister, just who the hell do you think you are, ordering us around like this?" the other bodyguard asked angrily.

"I think I'm the one with the loaded gun," Preacher said. "Now, do what I told you to do."

Reluctantly, but clearly with no choice, the men complied.

Turning his attention back to Blanton, Preacher saw that the banker was now holding a handkerchief to his nose. The slice on his nose was still bleeding, though not as profusely as before.

"I am Sylvanias Coopersmith's son," Preacher said. "I admit that I haven't been much of a son to him." Preacher was speaking as conversationally as if nothing had happened. "But I am his son nevertheless, and I'm here to pick up the paper you are holding against the farm."

"I'll get the paper for you," Blanton said. "You can have it. Just don't kill me."

Preacher shook his head. "No, you don't understand," he said. "I don't want you to give it to me. That would be the same as bank robbery and as soon as I left, you would just send the sheriff out there and take my father's farm. I'm not here to steal the paper, I'm here to pay off the loan. This is strictly a business operation."

"Is it your business to cut a man's nose off?" Blanton asked.

"Oh, but I didn't cut your nose off, though I could have if I had wanted to. So tell me, Blanton, are we going to talk business or not?"

Blanton pulled the handkerchief away from his nose. The bleeding had stopped, though there was quite a bit of blood on his face and the front of his shirt and vest. Blanton studied the handkerchief for a moment, as if unable to believe this had happened to him in his own bank. Finally, he looked up at Preacher.

"You do understand, don't you, that the entire amount is due? That includes principal, interest, and transfer charges."

"Transfer charges? What are transfer charges?" Preacher asked.

"There were expenses involved with transferring all of the loans from the previous mortgage holder over to me," Blanton explained.

"Seems to me like that would fall under the cost of doing business. By rights those are your costs, not the costs of your borrowers."

"All right. You are the one holding the gun. If you say no transfer charges, then there are no transfer charges."

Again, Preacher shook his head. "No, if these transfer charges are part of it, then I'll pay them as well. I told you, I intend for this to be all legal and proper. How much does my pa owe you?"

Blanton opened a drawer and pulled out a file. "It looks like your father, and I see here that your brother Morgan has signed as well, owes this bank a total of six hundred and twenty-seven dollars. "You have six hundred dollars and twenty-seven dollars on you, do you, Mr. Preacher?"

"I have these bank drafts," Preacher replied. Preacher showed him Blanton six documents, drawn for one hundred dollars each. "And I have twenty-seven dollars in cash," he added.

Blanton shook his head. "You don't have six

hundred dollars. What you have are bank drafts, and they aren't worth the paper they are printed on unless you can get a bank to honor them."

"These drafts are drawn against the River Bank of St. Louis," Preacher said. "Any bank in the country will honor them."

Closing the file, Blanton returned it to the drawer from which it had come. "I have no intention of honoring them," he said cryptically. "Unless, of course, you force me to honor them. As I said earlier, you are the man with the gun, and I never argue with a man who is holding a gun on me."

Preacher stared at Blanton, so angry with the fat man that his temple began to throb. Blanton was a quick learner. He had already learned how to play Preacher against himself. By saying that the only way he would honor the drafts would be for Preacher to force him to do so, he meant that he was inviting Preacher to take the deed by force. That was something Preacher had already said he would not do, because a deed taken by force, even in exchange for valid bank drafts, would be reported to the sheriff as soon as Preacher left.

"Very well, I will find a bank to honor it, and I'll bring cash."

Despite the wounded nose, Blanton actually allowed a smile to play across his face. He believed that he was in control now. This was business, and nobody was better at business than Klyce Blanton.

"You go find a bank, Mr. Preacher, or Cooper-smith . . . whatever you are calling yourself," Blanton said. "But when you do find one, understand this. I want the money in gold coin. I'm not interested in paper."

"Why not? I know that you deal in paper money," Preacher said.

"It is my option to ask for payment to be rendered in gold," Blanton said. "And that is what I intend to do, unless you force me to do otherwise." Blanton continued to play the hand he had been dealt. He knew, now, that Preacher wasn't going to force him into any deal that might later compromise the transaction. "So, if you want your papa's loan back, you are going to have bring me six hundred twenty dollars in gold," Blanton said. He snorted what might have been a chuckle. "You can bring me the seven dollars in paper money."

"I'll be back," Preacher said as he left the office.

Blanton followed Preacher to the door of his office, then stood there and watched as Preacher left the bank.

"You two worthless pieces of shit can get up now," Blanton said dismissively, speaking to his bodyguards, who were still sitting on the floor over in the corner of his office.

The two men stood and retrieved their guns.

"I'm going after the son of a bitch," Colby said, starting toward the door. "I'll teach him to treat me this way."

"No," Blanton said, holding his hand out to stop him. "You and McDougal follow him, but don't do anything until he gets the money."

"Then what?" Colby asked.

"I don't want him to make it back to the bank with it."

"What do you want us to do?"

"I don't want him to make it back to the bank with the money," Blanton said again, this time more pointedly than before.

"All right," Colby said.

# FIFTEEN

Preacher had no intention of letting Blanton take the farm away from his father. If the bank demanded cash money in order to retire the debt, then Preacher would come up with the cash. Whatever it took to get control of the farm returned to his father, Preacher intended to do.

The first requirement would be to find a bank that would honor the drafts from the River Bank of St. Louis. That in itself should not be hard, though it might be somewhat more difficult to find a bank that would pay in gold coin, rather than paper money.

This was Preacher's original home place, but he had grown to adulthood somewhere else. Because of that, he really knew very little about this area. In order to find a bank that would meet all the requirements, he would have to have help from someone, and he knew exactly who that someone would be. He walked down the street to visit with his brother-in-law.

Preacher thought his brother-in-law's establishment would be closed at this time of the morning, so he was surprised to see that Vaughan Roberts had already opened the Riverman's Inn for business. When he stepped inside, Vaughan looked up at him from behind the bar. Vaughan smiled, and called a greeting.

"Good morning, brother-in-law."

"Good morning," Preacher replied. He looked around the Inn, and saw that there were several people sitting at the tables.

"I wouldn't have expected you to have this many customers at this time of day," Preacher said. "Seems a little early to be drinking, doesn't it?"

Vaughan chuckled. "Not if you're drinking coffee," he replied.

"Coffee?"

"In the afternoon and at night, we are what some may call a tavern. But you notice we call it an inn, not a tavern, so we open in the morning and have quite a brisk breakfast trade. A lot of men, especially the bachelors, come in here for coffee and strudel. Your sister makes the best strudel in the county, and has proven it by winning prizes at the county fair."

"I didn't know that about her," Preacher said. "Actually, I'm ashamed to say, I know nothing about her, or any of the rest of my family."

"You have a wonderful family, I'm happy to say."

"Tell me about them," Preacher said. "Last night, I'm afraid that all I did was fill everybody in on where I've been and what I've done for the last fifteen years."

"All right, I'll start with your sister Betty. She was a schoolteacher until she got married, and she was a very good one. But as I'm sure you know, the school board has a strict rule against teachers being married so when she and Jim got hitched, she had to give up her job. There were a lot of disappointed families in the area, families whose older sons or daughters had been in Miss Coopersmith's class, and who wanted their younger children to have her as well.

"Betty's husband, Jim, publishes a newspaper, and even the governor has read and commented on some of his editorials. There are some who think Jim should run for office, but he insists that he can do more good as a newspaperman by, in his words, 'being the watchdog of the public.'

"Your brother Morgan, like your father, is a farmer. He works hard, is honest in his dealings with others, and there is no finer man in the county. His wife, Ann, happens to be my first cousin, so if I tell you what a wonderful person she is, you'll just say I'm being prejudiced."

"No, I would say who has a clearer idea than you," Preacher replied. "Thank you for filling me in on all of them, Vaughan. But I must say that, after seeing how well they all turned out, it's clear to me that I am the black sheep of the family," Preacher said. He was only half-jesting when he made the comment.

"Oh, I wouldn't say that," Vaughan said.

"I know they were all shocked to see me just drop in out of the blue the way I did."

"They may have been shocked—who wouldn't be to have you suddenly show up after such a long time. But I'll tell you this. I know they were all very happy to see you," Vaughan said. "Oh, where are my manners? Would you like some coffee?"

"Yes, thank you, that would be good. And one of my sister's pastries," he added with a smile. "I left the house before breakfast this morning."

A moment later, Vaughan served him.

Preacher took a bite of his sister's strudel. "Ummm, tell Tess this is very good."

"You can tell me yourself," Tess said, appearing in the door from the kitchen. She was wearing an apron upon which there was a light dusting of flour. An errant strand of hair hung down across her eyes, and when she brushed it back, she left a smudge of flour on her cheek.

"All right, I will tell you," Preacher said. "This is very good."

"Thank you," Tess replied. Then, in a more troubled tone of voice, she asked, "Arthur, what are you doing here? You aren't leaving again so soon, are you?"

"Not just yet," Preacher said.

"I'm glad to hear that. And don't think I'm not happy to see you, but I think you should spend more time with Mama and Papa."

"I will," Preacher said. "It's just that I had some business to take care of with Klyce Blanton."

"Klyce Blanton? You are doing business with that disagreeable man?" Tess asked. "Has Papa told you about the loan on the farm?"

"Yes."

"Everything was going just fine until Blanton bought the bank and began foreclosing on all the farmers. Why did he have to go sticking his nose into everyone else's business?"

"Some people are just that way, I suppose. But I do think that Blanton will be more careful about where he sticks his nose from now on," Preacher said.

"What do you mean?"

"Nothing, I was just making conversation."

"What kind of business did you have with Klyce Blanton?" Tess asked.

"Mortgage business," Preacher said, without being more specific. "Vaughan, if you were going to use a bank other than Blanton's bank . . ."

"I do use a bank other than his," Vaughan replied quickly.

"You do? You mean there is another bank in town? Which one? Where is it?"

Vaughan shook his head. "No, I didn't mean to give you the wrong impression. It's not in Portsmouth. The bank I use now is the Ohio Bank for Savings, over in Alexandria."

"Alexandria? Yes, I remember passing it on the way here. It's about ten miles downriver, isn't it?"

"Yes. Alexandria isn't as large as Portsmouth, but it does have a good bank. In fact, since Klyce Blanton bought out the bank here in Portsmouth and turned a good bank into a bad one, a lot of our local folks are doing their business over in Alexandria."

"Who is the head of the bank over there? Do you know him personally?"

"Yes, I do know him. His name is Burt Rowe. He's a good man."

"Arthur, if you are going to go over there to try and arrange a loan for Papa, I can tell you right now it won't do you any good. Vaughan had a new loan all set up, but Papa wouldn't do it."

"Why not?"

"Because Papa says you can't borrow yourself out of debt."

"Yes, well, he is probably right. But that's not what I had in mind."

"What did you have in mind?"

"I plan to pay off Pa's note so that he has the farm free and clear."

Tess gasped. "Arthur! You have enough money to do that?"

"Yes, and I have it with me. But it's not in cash. It's all in bank drafts."

"Bank drafts are fine," Vaughan said. "Why bother to go over to Alexandria with them? Blanton is the one who is holding the note. Why don't you just do business directly with him?"

"Well, like I said, Blanton and I had a brief discussion about that very thing this morning," Preacher replied. "He says he won't honor the drafts, and it is his right not to do so."

"I guess I'm not all that surprised that he won't do it," Vaughan said. "I have believed all along that Blanton isn't really interested in having the note paid off. What he actually wants is the land. He's got his hands on several thousand acres of prime bottomland right now, and your father's land is as good as any piece of land in the entire county. It may be the best land in the county. I'm sure Blanton is just itching to add your pa's land to his holdings."

"Well, he may want Pa's land, but he's not going to get it," Preacher said.

"Arthur, does Papa know you are doing this?" Tess asked.

"No. And don't you tell him until it's already done. I'm afraid he would try to stop me."

"You are right about that. He absolutely would try to stop you," Tess said. "Papa is a proud man who won't accept a handout from anybody. Not even one of his own children."

"Believe me, Tess, when I tell you that this isn't a handout," Preacher said. "The way I look at it, this is just payment for all the hurt I've caused Ma and Pa . . . that I've caused all of you . . . over the years. I'm hoping that once it's done, Pa will look at it that way too."

Tess smiled. "He will," she said. "I'll talk to Betty and Morgan, and we'll make certain he sees it that way."

"Thanks."

Tess leaned across the counter and put her hand on Preacher's. He could smell the scent of cinnamon and the aroma of flour and brown sugar. For just a moment, it caused him to recall his youth. Many times over the past several years, on those long, lonely nights in the mountains, he would sometimes think of his family, and he couldn't think of his mother without recalling that homey aroma. It seemed right and good now that his sister would be carrying that on.

"You're a good man, Arthur," Tess said. "I was very young when you left, and I'm afraid I don't remember you all that clearly now. I've often wondered where you went and how you turned out. I'm glad you came back, just so we would know what a good man you really are."

Preacher chuckled self-consciously. "Don't get me wrong. I'm not a saint, Tess," he said. "I've done things that I wouldn't want Ma or Pa, or even you or Betty or Morgan, to know about."

"You went out on your own when you were twelve years old, Arthur," Tess said. "I've no doubt that you had to do some things to survive. But survive you have, and here you are today, offering to pay off the farm for Papa. Whatever you may have had to do in the past, you are a good man today, and I love you for it."

"Thank you, Tess. I appreciate that coming from you."

The scene of familial affection was interrupted by the boisterous entry of a customer.

"Woo-hoo," the customer said loudly, coming into the inn laughing and slapping himself on the knees.

"Good morning, Ed," Vaughan said. "What's gotten into you this early in the day?"

"Vaughan, pour me a cup of coffee and bring out one of your wife's strudels, and I'll tell you the funniest thing I've heard in a long time," Ed said, taking a seat at the bar.

Vaughan poured the cup of coffee, then set a precut piece of strudel in front of him. "All right, Ed, just what is this funny story?" he asked.

"You know that fella that bought out the bank? The high-and-mighty Klyce Blanton?"

"Yes, of course I know him," Vaughan said. "He is so disagreeable, he has made himself known all over town."

"Yes, sir, that's the one, all right. But you just wait till you hear what just happened to him."

"Wait a minute. Are you saying something happened to Klyce Blanton?" Vaughan asked, glancing with some apprehension toward Preacher.

"It sure did, and Cleetus Butrum seen it all happen, so, according to him, this is the gospel truth."

"What did happen?"

"Blanton got his comeuppance, that's what happened," Ed said. He took a bite of the strudel. "Ummm, Mrs. Roberts, every strudel I have here is better than the one I had the day before. How do you do that?"

"I just follow the same recipe my mama and grandmother used," Tess said. "Tell us what happened to Klyce Blanton."

By now both Tess and Vaughan were staring at Preacher, who seemed to find something interesting to study in his coffee.

"It seems like some feller come into the bank this mornin' to discuss somethin' with Blanton. Well, I reckon the discussion didn't go to the feller's likin', so he took out his knife, then without so much as a by your leave, took him a slice out of the side of Blanton's nose." Ed laughed. "Just like that," he said.

"What do you mean when you say he took him a

slice? Are you saying this man cut part of Blanton's nose off?" Vaughan asked.

"Well, no, not exactly," Ed clarified. He put his finger alongside his nose, then made a cutting motion. "He just sliced right through it. Leastwise, that's what Cleetus is sayin'."

"And Cleetus is saying that all this took place in the bank?" Vaughan asked.

"Yes, in the bank. Right there in Blanton's office, accordin' to Cleetus," Ed said. He took another swallow of coffee, enjoying his moment of being the center of all attention.

"What about Colby and McDougal?" Vaughan asked. "They don't strike me as being the kind of men who would just stand there and watch all that happen without doing something about it. I thought they never left his side. Where were they when this was all going on?"

"Well, sir, accordin' to Cleetus, they was right there in the bank at the time and seen everything that happened."

"They saw it, but they didn't try to stop it?"

"Oh, yeah, they tried," Ed replied with a chuckle. "That's the best part," he said. "They did try, but accordin' to Cleetus, this here fella handled the two of 'em like they was no more'n babies. Had 'em both sittin' on the floor, he did, starin' at the wall, like the way teachers sometimes do with their dunces."

"You don't say," Vaughan said. Now the apprehension in his face was gone, and he looked at

Preacher with awe in his eyes and a smile on his lips.

"Chris Dumey seen Blanton a while ago and he said Blanton's nose was all red, with a purple scar where the cut was. The scar wasn't all that big, but you could sure see where it was. No, sir, I don't reckon the high-and-mighty Mr. Blanton is going to be so high-and-mighty anymore.

"So," Tess said to her brother. She chuckled quietly. "Klyce Blanton is going to be more careful about where he sticks his nose, is he?"

"That might be the wisest thing for him to do," Preacher replied.

Ed overheard Tess and Preacher, and though he didn't make the connection that Preacher was the one he was talking about, he did make the connection that the remark about the nose. He laughed out loud. "He's going to be more careful about where he sticks his nose," he said. "Yes, I reckon he is, all right." Ed laughed again. "That's a good one, that is. I'll have to remember that while I'm tellin' this story."

Finishing his coffee and strudel, Preacher stood. "I think I'd better be going. Tell me, Vaughan, can I rent a horse at the livery?"

"No need for you to be renting a horse when I can lend you one of mine," Vaughan said. "And I guarantee you, you'll be better mounted on my horse than you would if you rented."

"Thanks, I appreciate that," Preacher said.

"Also, before you leave, I'll write a letter of introduction to Mr. Rowe. That might be helpful to you in case he has any questions about why you want gold instead of paper for the bank drafts."

"Yes, thank you, Vaughan, that would be a big help," Preacher said.

tell it, or just ask questions about who put
gold coins on it? Just put on the bank drafts.

"Do you have questions that would be a little bit more..."

# SIXTEEN

It took Preacher less than an hour to reach Alexandria. Armed with the letter Vaughan had written, as well as the letter Constable Billings had given him back in St. Louis, he presented himself to Burt Rowe, the head of the bank.

Burt read both letters, then returned them. "They are good letters," he said. "They speak well of your honesty and integrity. Now, what can I do for you, sir?"

"I need to cash these bank drafts," Preacher said. "I need six hundred dollars in cash."

"Certainly, I see no problem with that," Rowe said. "Step over to the teller's cage, I'll instruct him to honor the drafts."

"I'll need the money in gold coin," Preacher added.

Rowe scratched his chin for a moment. "Gold coin?"

"Yes."

"Why gold coin? We issue United States Bank promissory notes. They are as good as gold everywhere."

"As good as gold isn't gold," Preacher said. He

sighed. "I don't mean to be picky, Mr. Rowe. But I'm paying off the mortgage on my father's farm. Klyce Blanton holds the paper, and he is demanding payment in gold in order to release it."

"I see," Rowe said, nodding his head. He sighed. "Blanton is the kind of man that gives bankers a bad name. Very well, Mr. Coopersmith, I'll honor the drafts with gold coin. I'll even put them in a bag for you."

"That would be helpful," Preacher said.

As Rowe searched for a cloth bag, Preacher happened to glance toward the wall, where there hung several posters. One poster in particular caught his attention, and he walked over for a closer look. As he examined it, he felt a surge of anger and determination.

*WANTED FOR*
*MURDER*
*DEAD OR ALIVE*
*Murderer Is*
*Missing His*
*Left Ear*

Burt Rowe came over to him then, bringing the cloth bag and the money. "Here is your money," he said, counting out the gold coins in front of him. When he counted out the full amount, he dropped the coins into the bag and handed the bag to Preacher.

"I saw you looking at that," he said, pointing to the poster.

"Yes. What do you know about this?"

"Terrible thing, that," the banker said. He then proceeded to tell the story of Billy and Suzie Potter finding their parents dead on the floor.

"They were murdered, both of 'em. Billy chased him with a pitchfork, but the man was mounted and rode away."

"How were Mr. and Mrs. Potter killed? Did the murderer slit their throats?"

"Yes," Rowe answered. He squinted. "Say, how did you know that?"

"Because that's the way he works."

"That's the way who works?"

"Ben Caviness. Could you tell me where the sheriff's is located?" Preacher asked. "I may have some information for him."

"Sheriff Wallace's office is just across the street, down on the corner," Rowe answered. "You can't miss it, it's the only brick building in that block."

Preacher took the bag of coins from Rowe. "Thank you very much for your help," he said, holding the bag up.

"You're welcome."

Sheriff Wallace, a gray-haired man of about fifty, was sitting at his desk, filling his pipe with tobacco, when Preacher came into his office. He looked up at Preacher with curiosity.

"Yes, sir, mister, something I can do for you?" the sheriff asked.

"Sheriff Wallace, my name is . . . " Preacher

started to identify himself as Preacher, but thought of the letter his brother-in-law had written for him, so he used his real name. "Art Coopersmith. I wonder if I could speak to you for a moment."

"Sure thing, Mr. Coopersmith. What do you have on your mind?"

"First, I'd like to show you this," Preacher said, handing Wallace the letter Constable Billings had written for him, appointing him his temporary deputy. The sheriff read it, then handed the letter back. "This letter calls you Preacher."

"It's a name some folks call me," Preacher said. He showed the sheriff his letter from Vaughan.

"All right, Preacher, or Mr. Coopersmith, whichever name you prefer. This first letter says you are a deputy in pursuit of a criminal and it asks for my cooperation. I'll be glad to cooperate with you all I can, but we are a pretty small town and I know everyone here. So I can tell you for a fact that the fella you are looking for, this"—Wallace glanced at the letter again—"Ben Caviness, isn't in Alexandria."

"He probably isn't," Preacher said. "But I believe he was here."

"What makes you think that?"

"I was just in the bank and noticed that you have a dodger posted on the wall. You had a murder take place here recently, committed by a man with only one ear."

"Yes, he killed Hiram and Emma Potter."

"I'm pretty sure that may the same man I'm looking for. Mr. Rowe said that the Potters' son and daughter saw the man."

"Yes, they did."

"I wonder if I could speak with the boy and his sister."

"Yes, I'm sure they'll talk to you," the sheriff replied. "Are you mounted?"

"I am."

"Let me saddle my horse and I'll ride out to the Potter farm with you."

At the Potter farm, Suzie was working in the garden while Billy was up on the roof of the house, replacing shingles. He had just reached for another shingle when he saw two riders approaching.

"Suzie, someone's coming," Billy called down from the roof.

Suzie looked up and used her hand to shield the sun from her eyes. "Who is it, can you tell?"

"Looks like the sheriff is one of them, but I don't know who the other man is."

"I'll make some lemonade," Suzie said. "No doubt they're hot after their ride."

Billy left his shingles on the roof, then climbed down the ladder. He was standing in front of the house when the two riders arrived.

"Sheriff Wallace," Billy said, greeting him.

"Billy, this is Mr. Coopersmith," Sheriff Wallace said. "But he goes by the name of Preacher."

"You're a pastor?"

"No. It's just a nickname people have hung on me. I'm comfortable with it now."

"I see you're keeping busy," Sheriff Wallace said, nodding toward the ladder.

"Yes, sir." Billy pointed to the roof of the house. "Pa kept tellin' me that we was goin' to have to put shingles on the roof this summer, but I kept puttin' 'im off 'cause I didn't want to do the work," he said. "But I put it off too long. Durin' the rain last week, the roof leaked somethin' awful."

The sheriff chuckled. "When shingles go bad, roofs will do that," he said. "How are you and your sister doing?"

"We're doin' all right. We miss Ma and Pa, but we're doin' just fine. Come on in, Suzie's makin' some lemonade."

"Thanks. Sounds good after a hot ride."

The three men went into the house, where Suzie greeted them with glasses of the confection.

"I just drew the water from the well, so they should be cool," she said, offering each of them a glass.

"Billy, Preacher thinks he knows who the fella is that killed your ma and pa," Sheriff Wallace said.

Billy looked at Preacher. "You know this man?" he asked.

"Yes. If he is who I think he is, he also killed a woman in St. Louis a few months ago," Preacher said. "I've been looking for him ever since."

"I wish you had found him before he got here," Suzie said, a tear sliding down her cheeks.

"I do too, miss," Preacher said. "And I'm very sorry for your loss. But I'll tell you this, if it's any comfort to you. I will find him."

"It won't bring Ma and Pa back."

"No, it won't do that," Preacher admitted.

"What's his name?" Billy asked.

"His name is Caviness. Ben Caviness," Preacher said. "He's a big man with dark hair and a crooked nose. And he's missing his left ear."

"That's him!" Suzie said, gasping.

"How'd he lose that ear?" Billy asked. "What he's got left is about the ugliest thing I've ever seen."

"The woman he killed had a dog with her. The dog chewed the ear off."

"Good for that dog," Billy said. "Too bad he didn't kill him."

"There were two men who attacked the woman," Preacher said. "And the dog did rip the throat out of the other one, killing him."

"Good."

"Billy, Sheriff Wallace said that you ran after Caviness, but he was riding."

"Yes. He was riding a bay," Billy said. "If he hadn't been mounted, he would be dead, because I would've caught up with him."

"He went that way, east," Suzie said, pointing. "Of course, he could have turned a different direction after he was out of sight. I think about that, about him still being out there, and sometimes I'm afraid at night, afraid that he may come back."

"I told her I wish he would come back," Billy said. "He got away from me once. If he comes back, he won't get away again."

"He won't be coming back," Preacher said. "He's heading east."

"You say that like you know it for a fact," Sheriff Wallace said.

"I do know it for a fact."

"Where is he heading, do you know?"

"He is going to Philadelphia."

After they finished their lemonade, Preacher and the Sheriff took their leave. As they left, the sheriff saw several rusting, iron washers lying on the ground under a tree, and he chuckled.

"You've got a lot of iron washers there, Billy," the sheriff said. "What are you planning on doing with them? Going into the iron washer business?"

"You remember, don't you, sheriff, how Dad use to run a float line out in the river for catfish?" Billy asked.

"Indeed I do," Wallace said. "I've had more'n one mess of your pa's fish."

"Well, he used these iron washers as weights for the fishing line. He liked to gather them up, but I don't have any use for them."

"You mean you don't fish?" Sheriff Wallace asked. "I figured, as good a fisherman as your pa was, you'd be out on the river too."

Billy shook his head. "No. Dad enjoyed it, but I don't. I wish I did enjoy it. I think Dad would have appreciated it if I had gone fishing with him, but I never did. I just don't have the patience, I guess."

"What are you going to do with all these washers now?" Preacher asked.

"I don't know. Bury them, I guess."

"I'll give you two dollars for the lot of them," Preacher offered.

Billy smiled broadly. "What? You'll give me two dollars for this?"

"For the whole pile," Preacher said. "What do you say?"

"I say that you've got yourself a deal!"

Preacher gave Billy two dollars, then scooped up all the washers and put them in his hat.

"What are you going to do with all them things?" the sheriff asked.

"I don't know," Preacher replied. He smiled. "Maybe I'll go fishing."


Billy and Suzie watched the two men ride away.

"I wish I was going with him," Billy said.

"Why?"

"I think he is going to catch up with this man Caviness. And when he does, I'd like to be there."

Suzie shivered. "Not I," she said. "I never want to see him again. And I don't know why you would want to."

"There's something about this man that tells me that when he does catch up with Ben Caviness, he is going to kill him," Billy said. "And I would like to be there when that happens."

"You mean you could watch something like that?" Suzie asked.

Billy spat on the ground, then started back toward the ladder to resume his work on the roof.

"Watch it?" he said. "I could do it myself."

# SEVENTEEN

Colby and McDougal knew that Preacher would have to go to Alexandria in order to find a bank that would honor the bank drafts, so, even as Preacher was in the Riverman's Inn, Blanton's two bodyguards were on their way to Alexandria. They got there ahead of Preacher and waited in the saloon, taking a table near the window so they could keep an eye on the bank, which was located just across the street.

"You think he'll get the gold?" McDougal asked.

"I reckon he will," Colby said. He chuckled. "But he ain't goin' to keep it long, seein' as how we'll just meet him out on the road somewhere between here and Portsmouth and relieve him of that burden."

"Yeah, well, if it was up to me, I'd do more than take the money from him. I'd kill the son of a bitch," McDougal said.

"And you'd get hung for it too," Colby replied. "Hell, you'd get us both hung."

"I just don't like the way he done us back in Portsmouth."

"Me neither. I never seen anyone move as fast as he did."

"Yeah, well, iffen he hadn't already pinned you

to the wall with that knife, I would'a had a shot at him," McDougal said. "I could'a kilt him then, and it would'a been self-defense."

"Why didn't you?"

" 'Cause I told you, you was in the way."

"So you say. But truth to tell, when you come runnin' into the room, he was already standin' there with his gun draw'd, pointin' right at your innards."

"That's the truth," McDougal admitted. "Wait a minute, ain't that him comin' up the road there?"

Colby looked out the window in the direction McDougal was pointing.

"Yeah," he said. "That's him, all right. Couldn't be nobody else, dressed like he is, with them buckskins and that hat."

They watched Preacher ride the length of the street, then stop in front of the Ohio Bank for Savings. Dismounting, he tied his horse off, then went inside.

"Mr. Blanton was right. He come right here to this bank for his gold, just like he said he would."

They waited for several minutes, drinking beer and watching the bank and the street, until they saw Preacher coming back out of the bank, carrying a sack.

"Look at that there sack he's carryin'. Looks like he got the gold," McDougal said.

"Yeah, but he won't keep it very long," Colby said. "I'm going to enjoy takin' it from him almost as much as I would killin' him."

To their surprise, Preacher didn't remount. Instead, he walked across the street, still carrying the sack of gold. They watched as he went into the small brick building that sat on the corner.

"What the hell?" McDougal said. "He's gone into the sheriff's office."

"Yeah," Colby said. "The question is, what's he gone in there for?"

"Maybe he's going to have the sheriff ride back to Portsmouth with him to guard the money," McDougal suggested.

"No, a sheriff ain't goin' to do somethin' like that. He'd have to hire him a private guard."

"Well, maybe he's going to the sheriff to find out where he can come by someone like that."

"Yeah, that could be, I suppose," Colby said. "But to tell you the truth, the way that fella handled himself, don't seem to me like he would be a'needin' no private guards."

They waited another few minutes, watching the front of the sheriff's office. Then Preacher and Sheriff Wallace came out together.

"Wait a minute, this ain't no guardin'. This is somethin' else," Colby said.

Colby was right. When Preacher and Sheriff Wallace left the sheriff's office, they rode, not toward Portsmouth, but in the opposite direction.

"What do you reckon this is all about?" McDougal asked.

"I don't know," Colby replied. "But I reckon about the only thing we can do is trail 'em and find out what they're up to."

Colby and McDougal trailed Preacher and the sheriff, always remaining some distance away so they could keep up with what was going on without compromising their presence. When they saw Preacher and the sheriff heading toward a small farmhouse, they dismounted and moved their horses into a clump of trees so they could watch without being observed.

"You know who I think that is?" Colby said after a moment of watching Preacher and the sheriff in conversation with the person who had climbed down from the roof of the house to meet them.

"Who?"

"I think that's the Potter boy," Colby said. "You mind, it was in the paper back in Portsmouth. He's the one somebody killed his parents."

"Yeah, I remember that. But what's he's talkin' to Coopersmith for?" McDougal asked.

"I don't know, but as long as the sheriff's there too, there's not much we can do but just wait and watch," Colby said.

"So what do we do now?" McDougal asked.

Colby stroked his jaw for a moment as he tried to determine what their next move should be. Finally, he reached a decision.

"Get mounted," he said. "We're headin' back to Portsmouth."

"What?" McDougal replied in protest. "Didn't you say we was goin' to take that gold offen him?"

"Yes, and we are," Colby said. "But not while the sheriff is around. I don't know what all this is about, but I got me a feelin' that it don't have nothin' to do with us. So, I figure the sheriff will go back to his office in Alexandria, while Coopersmith takes the gold back to Portsmouth. Don't forget, he wants to pay off the loan so he can get his pappy's farm back."

"Yeah, all right," McDougal said, remounting. "Let's go."

Leaving Preacher and the sheriff in conversation with Billy Potter, Colby and McDougal started back toward Portsmouth. Almost exactly halfway between the two towns, the road made a curve around a rather large outcropping of rocks.

"Right here," Colby said, pointing to the rocks. "It's perfect. We can see him comin', and he won't see us."

Dismounting, they ground-hobbled their horses, then took up a position that allowed them see nearly a mile down the road.

They waited.

Colby slapped at a fly.

McDougal got up.

"Where you goin'?" Colby asked.

"To take a piss," McDougal answered.

Colby had turned his attention back to the road when he heard McDougal.

"Woo-wee, look at this," McDougal said.

"Look at what?"

"I'm tryin' to piss this here grasshopper offen a weed, but the little son of a bitch just grabbed hold and is hangin' on," McDougal said.

"McDougal, you are one strange shit, did you know that?" Colby asked.

McDougal came back to the rock, buttoning up his pants as he did so. "See anything yet?"

"No," Colby replied. "If I had seen something, I would've told you."

They waited for several more minutes. Then Mc-Dougal spoke again.

"Here he comes."

"And the sheriff ain't with 'im," Colby said. He pulled a hood from his saddlebag and slipped it on over his head. "Let's get the job done."

Preacher was riding back to Portsmouth when two men suddenly appeared in front of him, jumping out from behind a rock. Both men were wearing hoods over their faces, with nothing but tiny holes for their eyes. Both were armed and they had their pistols, charged and cocked, leveled at him.

Had it not been for the fact that they were armed, Preacher might have laughed at them. The hoods over their heads did absolutely nothing to conceal their identities. Colby and McDougal were still wearing the same clothes they'd had on in Blanton's bank earlier this morning. Preacher put up his hands.

"All right, my hands are up," Preacher said. "What do you want?"

"I want you to untie that there money bag from your saddle pommel and hand it over here," one of the men said, his voice somewhat muffled by the hood.

Slowly, Preacher did as he was told, handing it to the one who had extended his hand. The robber tied the sack to his own saddle pommel.

"Hand over your gun too," that same robber said.
Preacher gave the robber his pistol.

"Now, get down from your horse," the robber added, making a motion with his gun.

"What you goin' to do with him?" the other robber asked.

"This is a tricky son of a bitch," the first robber said. "I aim to make sure we get away." He took the horse's reins. "Let's go!" he said.

Preacher stood in the road and watched as the two robbers left with his horse, moneybag, and pistol. Inexplicably, he laughed. Then, with no choice but to walk, he resumed his journey back to Portsmouth.

He had gone about a mile and a half when he saw his brother-in-law's horse standing alongside the road, calmly cropping grass. He didn't know if the horse had bolted, or if the robbers had let it go. Either way, the horse was clearly a welcome sight.

"Whoa, boy," Preacher said, speaking gently to him. He went over to the horse and patted him on the face a couple of times, then remounted and continued his journey as if nothing had happened.

Preacher's first stop when he returned to Portsmouth was the bank. Going inside, he headed straight for Blanton's office.

"Here, sir, you can't just go barging into Mr. Blanton's office," one of the bank employees called out to him as Preacher walked by the teller's cage.

"Sure I can," Preacher replied airily. "Blanton and I are old friends now, and he is expecting me."

Pushing the door open to Blanton's office, Preacher saw the angry banker staring down at the top of his desk. Standing to either side of Blanton, with perplexed and frustrated expressions on their faces, were Colby and McDougal. On the desk in front of Blanton was a cloth bag imprinted with the words "Ohio Bank For Savings." It was the same bag Preacher had gotten from Burt Rowe at the bank in Alexandria, and the same bag he had given up to the highwaymen.

Also on the top of Blanton's desk were several of the rusting iron washers Preacher had bought from Billy Potter.

"Good afternoon, Mr. Blanton," Preacher said cheerfully. He was carrying another sack, and from this sack, he began pulling gold coins and putting them in little piles on the top of Blanton's desk.

"I believe you asked for payment in gold?" Preacher said.

"What the . . . " Colby said with a sputter. He pointed to the gold coins Preacher was stacking up. "Where the hell did you get that gold?"

"Why, you know exactly where I got it, Mr. Colby. You and McDougal were sitting in the saloon across from the bank when I cashed the bank drafts."

"What? How'd you know we was there?" McDougal asked, sputtering in surprise.

"Shut up, McDougal," Blanton said with an

angry snarl. "Are you that damn stupid that you haven't figured this out yet?"

"What?" McDougal asked, still clearly confused.

"And now, Mr. Blanton, if you please, I'd like the mortgage to Pa's place," Preacher said.

With an angry look and a snort of disgust, Blanton got up from his desk and walked over to a cabinet, where he jerked open a drawer. After rifling through a few papers, he pulled one out, then came back and slapped it down on the desk in front of Preacher.

"Here it is," he said. "Take the damn thing and be damned."

Preacher looked at the document for a moment, then handed it back to Blanton.

"What now?"

"I would appreciate it if you would write, on the bottom, 'This debt is paid in full,' then sign your name, please."

Blanton did as Preacher asked, signing his name in a large, illegible scrawl, before returning the paper to Preacher.

Preacher folded the paper carefully and put it in his pocket. Then, looking at the top of Blanton's desk, he asked, almost conversationally, "Are you going fishing?"

"Fishing?" Blanton replied.

Preacher pointed to the pile of washers on Blanton's desk.

"Yes," Preacher said. "I'm told those make very good weights. And since you aren't a mechanic, I can't think of any other reason you might have them on your desk."

"Fishing weights?" Blanton growled angrily. He swept several of them from his desk and, as they clattered and clanged to the floor, he looked over at McDougal and Colby. "You brought me fishing weights?"

"How were we supposed to know?" McDougal asked. "They were in a bank bag and . . ."

"McDougal, shut the hell up!" Colby shouted.

"Oh, yeah," McDougal said, growing quiet.

Preacher began stacking the gold coins up on the desk. When he was finished with the coins, he piled up an equally high stack of the washers right alongside. Then he put his finger on each one of them.

"You shouldn't be so hard on them, Blanton," Preacher said. "When you stop and think about it, if you put a bunch of iron washers in a bank sack, almost anyone might think they were gold coins."

"You've got the deed to your father's farm now," Blanton said between clenched teeth. "I want you to take it, get the hell out of my office, and stay out."

"It's been a pleasure doing business with you," Preacher said with a little laugh.

"I just wish I could've been a fly on the wall whenever ole Klyce Blanton dumped out that sack and what he thought was gold turned out to be nothing but iron washers," Preacher's brother, Morgan, said with a laugh.

The others laughed as well.

It was a gala dinner, with Preacher's mother cooking everything she remembered as her oldest son's favorite. The whole family was laughing and talking, celebrating the fact that, once more, the farm was owned free and clear.

Despite the celebratory atmosphere, though, Preacher's father seemed unusually subdued. After a while, he excused himself from the table, then went outside.

"What's wrong with your pa?" Betty's husband, Jim, asked.

"Nothing, he'll be all right," Betty said.

"Sylvanias is a proud man," Preacher's mother said of her husband. "When the rest of us learned what a wonderful thing Arthur was doing, we went to him and begged him to accept this."

"We finally convinced him," Morgan said. "But it's not sitting well with him."

"He'll get over it," Preacher's mother said to her son, reaching across the table to pat him on the back of his hand. "He just needs a little time, that's all."

"Hey, Vaughan, tell me again about Blanton's nose," Morgan said.

Although he had already told the story Ed was spreading around town, he retold it, adding his own embellishments.

"Whatever he looks like now, it has to be an improvement," Tess said, and once again the dining room echoed with laughter.

With the others were engaged in animated conversation, Preacher left. A moment later, he pushed the front door open, then stepped out onto the porch. He saw his father standing against the porch railing, looking down toward the river.

The air was soft and warm, and filled with the sounds of the night: frogs calling for their mates, insects, and night birds. A mule brayed in the barn. Fireflies winked over the rolling land between the house and the river.

"Peaceful out here," Preacher said.

"Yes," Sylvanias answered.

Preacher walked over to stand beside him. A streak of light raced across the sky.

"There's a falling star," Preacher said.

"They tell me stars are really bright out in the mountains," Sylvanias said. "Is that so?"

"Yes, sir," Preacher said. "Sometimes you get the idea you could just about reach up and pull one down."

Sylvanias was quiet for another moment, and Preacher didn't intrude into the silence. Finally, he spoke again.

"Art, I don't want you to think I'm not grateful for what you did," he said. "Paying off the mortgage and all."

"I don't think that," Preacher said.

"But it's hard for me to accept somethin' I didn't earn."

"Pa, when a man has sons, he expects his sons to be a help to him until they get out on their own. Maybe they start small, picking up a few things here and there, then feeding the stock. But the time comes when the son has to carry a full share of the load.

"That happened with Morgan. He came of age

and started carrying his full share of the load. But I never did. I left home, and I deprived you of what you had every right to expect. I know that paying off this mortgage doesn't nearly pay you back for all that I owe you, but I hope it helps."

Again, Sylvanias was silent. "You'll be going on tomorrow?" he asked.

"Yes, sir," Preacher said.

"Chasing the man who killed your woman."

"Turns out he also killed the Potters, over in Alexandria," Preacher said.

Sylvanias nodded. "Yes, I remember reading about that in Jim's newspaper. I reckon stopping someone like him is a noble enough deed. Just be careful. Even if you aren't going to stay here, it's nice knowing you are alive somewhere."

"I'll be careful," Preacher promised.

"Preacher, you'll always have a place to come to. I want you to know that."

"Thanks, Pa. I do know it, and I take comfort in it."

It did not escape Preacher's notice that his father called him Preacher. In so doing, Preacher knew his father was letting him know that he had forgiven his young son Arthur for leaving home so long ago, and now accepted Preacher on his own terms.

For the first time in fifteen years, Preacher was absolutely at peace with himself over that rash decision he had made while still a boy.

# EIGHTEEN

*Philadelphia*

Caviness had thought that St. Louis was a big city, but Philadelphia was ten times bigger. He had never seen as much activity as he saw when he arrived in the City of Brotherly Love.

He saw a lot of strange things, such as long wagons with several windows down each side, filled with seats on which people entered and left, seemingly without rhyme or reason. Someone referred to the wagon as an omnibus, and it was pulled by a single horse along rails of iron.

In addition to the omnibuses, there were literally hundreds of wagons and carriages of all sizes and descriptions, their iron-rimmed wheels ringing and the shod hooves clattering on the cobblestone-paved streets. Often, several of the wagons and carriages would congregate at a street intersection and some of the drivers would blow through the trumpets they carried, while others shouted impatiently as they tried to disentangle themselves.

In addition to the wheeled vehicles, there were also men on horseback, though there were not nearly as many riders as there were drivers and passengers of the wheeled vehicles. Even the walks, alongside the streets, were filled with people, rushing to and fro, pushing, crowding as they hurried to wherever they were going.

Caviness saw a man standing on the corner, waiting to cross the street, and he rode over to him.

"Hey, you," Caviness said. "Where at can I find me a man by the name of Epson?"

"I have no idea," the man replied.

"Epson," Caviness said again, thinking that if he repeated the name, the man might be able to answer.

"No doubt there are scores of Epsons in Philadelphia," the man said. "And even if I knew any of them, which I don't, I would have no idea which one you are talking about."

At that moment there was a break in the traffic, and the man walked quickly across the street.

Caviness inquired of several more people, with an equal lack of success. Then, as he was riding along slowly, taking everything in, he heard a trumpet being blown behind him. The horn was so close and so loud that it made his horse jump. He had to jerk back on the reins to keep the animal under control. Looking around, he saw a carriage in which four well-dressed men were riding.

The men were sitting back in the passenger section of the carriage, engaged in animated conversation, oblivious to the traffic around them. But the driver, a large, liveried black man, was acutely aware of what was going on. He was the one who had blown the horn, and now he was standing up, shaking the trumpet at Caviness.

"Mister, if you don't know what you are doing, get out of the road!" he shouted, angrily.

Caviness was shocked. He had never heard a black man talk to a white man in such a fashion, and he looked to the passengers in the carriage to see if they would remind their driver of his station.

To Caviness's surprise, they not only did not correct him, but one of them shouted out, "We're late, James. Get us through all this."

"Yes, sir," James replied. James picked up a whip and snapped it very close to Caviness's face. "Now, mister, do you get out of the way, or do I whip you out of the way?"

With an angry glare at the black driver, Caviness moved his horse to one side. As the carriage passed him by, Caviness heard one of the men laugh.

"Where did that oaf come from?"

Caviness continued to ride up and down the streets, asking about Epson. Most of the time, he got no response of any kind, and those who did reply said that they couldn't help him.

It was nearly noon, and as he rode by a few of the restaurants, he could smell the aroma of cooking food. The smells reminded him that he was hungry, but they also reminded him that he had no money.

Seeing a hitching rail, Caviness dismounted and tied off his horse.

"Mister, you can't leave your horse here," a fancy-dressed man told him.

"Why not?"

"Only members can tie their horses or park their carriages here."

"Only members of what?"

"Why, members of the Philadelphia Social Club, of course," the man replied haughtily.

"Are you a member?"

"Do I look like a member, dressed as I am?" The man was wearing a tri-corn hat, a red jacket with brass buttons, and yellow pants tucked down into highly polished brown boots.

"I don't know, you look pretty fancy-dressed to me," Caviness replied.

"I am sergeant at arms for the group," the man said. "This is my uniform."

"They got 'em somebody from the Army to look after things for them, do they? I never heard of such a thing. What do them folks do in that club?"

"The same thing as they do in any club," the sergeant at arms replied. "They drink, eat, socialize, discuss matters of importance."

"You don't say. Well, that sounds good to me. Especially the eatin' part. I think I'll join."

The sergeant at arms laughed out loud. "That's very funny."

"No, I'm serious, I'll join. Where do I go to join up with 'em?"

"You have to apply for membership, and you must have two sponsors who are already members. Then, when they vote on you, you must be unanimously accepted. If but one member blackballs you, you will not be allowed in. And if you are allowed in, then you must pay the entrance fee and the dues."

"How much is that?"

"If you have to ask, it is too much," the sergeant at arms said. "Now, please, take your horse and go somewhere else."

Grumbling, Caviness remounted and rode away. He had never heard of such a thing as a private club, but if they ate and drank, it sounded fine to him. Maybe Epson could tell him how to get in. Or maybe Epson already belonged to such a club. That fancy-dressed sergeant had told him that he would have to know someone who already belonged in order to be a member.

Two more times, Caviness attempted to tie off his horse, but he was run away both times, once because it was in front of someone's house . . . though the house was larger than any hotel Caviness had ever seen. The other time, he was told that the hitching rail was for customers only. He was beginning to wonder if there was anyplace in Philadelphia for a visitor to tie his horse.

Where the hell was Epson anyway? And how was he going to find him?

More important than finding Epson right now was getting something to eat. This wasn't like it was back in St. Louis, where he knew which households he could go to begging for food. Now, with his ear cut off, he made such a terrifying appearance that women were afraid of him. And it was his experience that women would have nothing to do with men who frightened them.

Caviness continued to ride through the city until he reached an area where there were far fewer people. There, he found a sapling, and at last was able to secure his horse.

Looking around, he saw that, though he was still in the city, this particular area had grass, shrubbery, and trees. It was actually a park, though "park" wasn't a term Caviness would have recognized.

Looking across the open area, he saw a man walking along a path. The path led down into a grove of trees, where it disappeared. Moving quickly, Caviness hurried down to those same trees and followed the man along the path. Within moments, the city seemed far away. So isolated were they, that they could have been in the middle of the deep woods somewhere. This was more to Caviness's liking.

Caviness knew he would not get a better opportunity than this. Taking out his knife, he moved quickly up the path until he saw, just ahead of him, the man he had seen earlier. Walking quickly but quietly, Caviness moved up on him so silently that his victim didn't even know Caviness was there until he felt a hand clamp down across his mouth.

Caviness pulled the knife across the man's throat, then dropped him to the ground. The man flopped around a few times, like a fish out of water, and died.

Looking around to make certain nobody had seen him, Caviness then bent down over the body and began searching his pockets. A moment later, he pulled out a wallet, and was gratified to see that it contained fourteen dollars in paper money.

"Well, now," Caviness said aloud. "It 'peers as if my luck is changin'."

Sticking the billfold into his own pocket, Caviness

hurried back to his horse, mounted, then rode to one of the restaurants. This time, when he tied off in front of the restaurant, he wasn't challenged.

### THIRD MURDER VICTIM FOUND
*Like Previous Two, Has Throat Cut*

Philadelphia is being besieged with a string of gruesome murders. In but two weeks, three of our finest and most promising gentlemen have been killed by an unknown assailant in a manner so foul as to defy description.

The most recent victim was Mr. B.G. Grant, age 31. Like the other two victims, Mr. Grant was found with his throat cut, in a part of the city that is less traveled. It is believed that the murderer lies in wait in these more remote locations, picking his victims at a time when no one else is around to offer assistance.

The constabulary force of Philadelphia is searching for this heinous killer, and asks all to be on the alert for anything suspicious. Our citizens are cautioned against finding themselves alone in such areas, lest the killer strike again.

Theodore Epson was reading the newspaper when an office boy approached his desk.

"Mr. Epson?"

Epson looked up from his paper. "Yes, Johnny, what is it?" he asked.

"Mr. Fontaine asks that you come to his office."

It had been some time since Fontaine had

mentioned anything to Epson about the matter in St. Louis, and Epson thought that the matter was closed. Then he remembered that Miller was going to St. Louis.

"Did he say what it was about?"

"No, sir, he didn't say."

"Tell me, do you know if Mr. Miller has returned from St. Louis?"

"Yes, sir, he has," the office boy replied. "He's in Mr. Fontaine's office now."

Once again, Epson felt a sense of apprehension. Had Miller found something incriminating during his trip to St. Louis?

"Are the other members of the board there as well?"

"No, sir. Just Mr. Fontaine and Mr. Miller," Johnny answered.

Epson breathed a sigh of relief. If none of the other board members were present, then it didn't seem very likely that anything was going to happen. Walking erect, as if he had nothing to worry about, Epson crossed the bank to Fontaine's office. He started to knock on the door, but was interrupted by Joel Fontaine's appointments clerk.

"Mr. Fontaine said for you to just go right in, sir," the appointments clerk said. "He and Mr. Miller are waiting for you."

"Thank you," Epson said.

He pushed the door open and, hesitantly, stepped into Fontaine's office.

"Come in, Mr. Epson, come in," Fontaine called. "You remember Mr. Miller?"

"Yes, of course," Epson said. "How was your trip to St. Louis?"

"Tiring," Miller replied. "And disagreeable. St. Louis may call itself a city, but in fact it is nothing more than a frontier town. They have few of the amenities of a real city."

"Have a seat, Mr. Epson," Fontaine said, pointing to a comfortable chair that was close to his desk. This was a much better sign than the last time he was in here, when he was forced to sit in a hard, straight-back chair that was purposely set apart from the others.

"Thank you," he said. Epson was still carrying the newspaper he had been reading, and he held it now, folded across his lap.

"Mr. Miller has a bit of disturbing news for us," Fontaine said.

"You have some disturbing news?" Epson leaned forward in his chair, once more feeling a sense of apprehension.

"Yes, well, disturbing in its content. Though in one way, I suppose it is good news for you. Though, not the way you would like to hear it, I'm sure."

"What is it? I don't understand what you are talking about."

"Mr. Miller, suppose you tell Mr. Epson what you told me."

"Yes. Well, as you know, Mr. Epson, it was my intention, when I reached St. Louis, to question this Miss Jennie, to see what I could find out about all these claims she has been filing against you."

"And did you interview her, sir?"

"No, I'm afraid that was not possible. When I arrived in St. Louis, I inquired about her at the bank, only to learn that she was dead."

"Dead? Jennie is dead?"

"Yes. She was murdered."

"Oh, my," Epson said.

"That means, of course, that the constant barrage of charges she has been lodging against you, whether spurious or valid, will stop."

"Yes, sir," Epson said. "And I assure you, sir, they were spurious."

"I'm sure that they were, though now we will really never know. At any rate, tragic though it might be, her demise is to your advantage," Fontaine said.

"Yes, sir, I suppose it is." Epson laughed weakly. "I suppose it is good that I did not go to St. Louis to answer these charges, for if I had, I would surely be a suspect now."

"That is so," Fontaine replied. "But since you were clearly here in Philadelphia when the poor girl was murdered, you are not under any suspicion."

"No, I wouldn't think that I am," Epson said, relief clearly showing in his voice.

"Do they know who did kill her?" Fontaine asked Miller.

"Seems she was attacked by two men, but one of them, a man by the name of Slater, was killed by her dog. They know there was another one, because they found his ear. Seems the dog chewed it off."

"Do they have any idea who the other one was?"

"They are looking for a man named Caviness," Miller said.

Epson gasped slightly. "Caviness?" he asked.

"Yes. Do you know him?"

"I, uh, know who he is," Epson replied. "He was a ne'er-do-well who hung around town. A one-time fur trapper who wasn't very good at it, as I recall. How do they know he was involved?"

"They don't know for sure, but it seems he and Slater had been seen together earlier that night, and Caviness hasn't been seen since."

"Terrible thing," Fontaine said, clucking and shaking his head.

"It is indeed," Miller agreed. "And one might say that the poor girl was murdered because St. Louis is such a wild frontier town that there is little law and less civil behavior. But I understand now that while I was gone, we had three murders in as many weeks right here in our own city of Philadelphia."

"Yes," Epson said. He held up the newspaper. "As a matter of fact, I've been reading about them."

"Ironically, the poor souls who died here were killed in just as gruesome a fashion as was the lady in St. Louis," Miller continued. "They died by having their throats cut. And that is exactly how the young lady of your acquaintance died."

"I respectfully ask that you not refer to her as a person of my acquaintance, since that suggests that there was a relationship when, clearly, none existed," Epson said.

"I'm sorry. I didn't mean to imply that you had a relationship with the lady," Miller explained.

"Woman," Epson corrected.

"I beg your pardon?"

"As I've explained before, the woman in question is, uh, that is, she was a prostitute. A common whore. It seems to me inappropriate to call a harlot a lady."

"Perhaps that is so," Fontaine replied. "But I would hope you could be a bit more generous in your comments about her now that the poor lady is dead."

Fontaine came down harder on the word "lady."

"After all," he continued, "her untimely death has cleared you of all suspicion."

"Yes, sir, it has indeed," Epson said, unable to prevent the smile from spreading across his face.

So great was Epson's relief over how things had turned out that he didn't even notice the disapproving look Fontaine and Miller exchanged.

"That is all, Mr. Epson. You may return to your work now," Fontaine said with a slight, dismissive wave of his hand.

"Very good, sir," Epson replied.

When Epson returned to his desk, he pulled out the newspaper and attempted to read, but though he tried hard, he was unable to finish the story. He couldn't keep his mind off the meeting he had just had with Fontaine and Miller.

Was he responsible for Jennie's death? He could be, he knew. In his last letter to Caviness he had been very specific about what he wanted. He'd wanted his troubles to go away, and he'd said exactly than in his letter.

But he had not been specific as to how he meant for Caviness to make those troubles go away.

It now appeared as if Caviness had decided that the only way to make that happen was by killing Jennie.

Epson felt a momentary twinge of regret over that. He did not consider himself a criminal, even though he had taken 950 dollars that didn't belong to him.

Some might call him a thief for that, but in his mind, a thief was someone who stole by force or stealth, and he had done neither. Although he had not come by his windfall of 950 dollars in what could be described as an honest way, he had not stolen it in any way that he would describe as theft. After all, the money had been dropped in his lap. He'd merely taken advantage of that, as he was sure any astute businessman would.

He was not a thief.

Nor was he a murderer.

He did not kill Jennie, though it now seemed certain that Caviness did. And if Caviness did kill her, it was surely in response to his specific instructions to make his "problems go away."

He wondered where Caviness was now. If, as Miller said, his ear had been chewed off, there was a good chance Caviness was dead somewhere. It would be hard to stop the bleeding in a wound like that. The wound could also putrefy. Either one could kill him.

# NINETEEN

When Preacher awoke, he got out of bed, walked over to the window of his hotel room, and looked out over the city of Philadelphia. Arriving by stagecoach after dark last night, he had gone to a hotel, deciding to start his search today.

There was a knock on his door and for a moment, he was startled by it. Who would be calling on him? Who even knew he was here?

"Breakfast," a muffled voice announced from the other side of the door, and Preacher relaxed. He remembered now that when he'd arrived last night, he'd been asked if he would like breakfast delivered to his room this morning.

Crossing the room quickly, Preacher opened the door to see a young black boy, no more than twelve years old, holding a tray. From somewhere in the back of his mind he knew that a tip was required, so handed the boy a coin.

"Thank you, sir," the boy said with a wide grin.

Preacher took the tray into his room, put it on a table, pulled up a chair, and began having his breakfast. He chuckled as he compared this breakfast, in a plush hotel room in a large Eastern city, with the breakfasts he had eaten in the wilderness over the last several years.

"I'd better watch myself," he said aloud as he reached for a jar of marmalade. "I could learn to like this awfully easily."

Even as he spoke the words, he knew that he couldn't really live like this. Already he was feeling restricted, and he missed the mountains that had become his home.

He also realized that he had better watch himself as far as speaking to himself was concerned. It was a habit he had developed in the wilderness, but that wasn't needed here. In a city the size of Philadelphia, he had plenty of opportunity to hear other voices and to speak to other people. There was no justification for speaking to himself, and if anyone heard him, they might think him crazy.

A newspaper had been delivered with his meal, and as Preacher put marmalade on his biscuit, he glanced through the paper. He had just raised the biscuit to take a bite when he read the headline over one of the articles.

## FOURTH VICTIM FOUND WITH THROAT CUT

Preacher read the story carefully, and by the time he finished both his breakfast and the newspaper, he was totally convinced that Ben Caviness was in Philadelphia. He was convinced of that fact because he was certain that Caviness was the Philadelphia murderer.

***

Preacher stood in front of a rather substantial-looking brick building looking up at the sign over the front door. The sign read PHILADELPHIA POLICE AGENCY.

Unlike St. Louis, which had a constable and a deputy, Philadelphia had a well-organized police agency, consisting of constables, wardens, and watchmen. The watchmen patrolled the city from "watch boxes," which were scattered throughout the town.

Preacher went inside, where he was met by a man who was wearing a domed hat with a badge.

"Yes, sir, can I help you?"

"I'd like to speak to whoever is in charge," Preacher said.

"That would be Chief Constable Dolan," the man said. "May I tell him what this is about?"

"Yes," Preacher said. "I think I know who is doing all the killings here."

"Do you now?" To Preacher's surprise, the man began filling his pipe.

"What is your name?" Preacher asked.

"I'm Constable Coleman," the man said as he tamped down the tobacco in the bowl of his pipe.

"Well, Constable Coleman, are you going to tell the chief constable that I would like to see him?" Preacher asked.

"And just who do you think is doing the killing?" Coleman asked.

"I'd rather give that information to the chief constable," Preacher replied.

Coleman lit his pipe, then drew several puffs, encircling his head with wreaths of smoke, before he responded.

"Well, now, here's the thing," Coleman said. "You are the tenth person to come in here with an idea as to who is doing the killing."

"I am?" Preacher replied, surprised by Coleman's comment. "Have that many people heard of Ben Caviness?"

Coleman had just started to take another puff of his pipe, but he pulled it away from his lips. Now the expression on his face changed to one of interest.

"Wait a minute," he said. "Do you really know who this is?"

"Well, I know Ben Caviness, I know that he has killed like this before, and I know he is in Philadelphia, because I followed him here."

"You followed him here?"

"From St. Louis," Preacher said.

Coleman studied Preacher for a moment longer. Then he said, "Wait here. I'll tell the chief constable that you would like to speak to him."

"Thank you."

A moment later, Coleman returned and escorted Preacher to a room in the back of the building.

"I'm Chief Constable Dolan," a tall, bewhiskered man said, extending his hand. "And you are?"

"Folks call me Preacher," Preacher said.

"Well, Preacher, Constable Coleman here tells me that you know who our murderer is."

"Yes, I do," Preacher said. "Or at least, I think I know."

"Well, which is it? You do know, or you think you know?" Coleman asked.

Preacher told them the story of his quest, beginning with the fact that he was a mountain man and fur trapper who had come back to St. Louis when he learned that a female friend of his had had her throat cut by a man named Ben Caviness.

"She was killed in the same way as the four people in this city were killed," Preacher said. "That is, if the details in the newspaper article are correct." He thumped the newspaper with his thumb.

"And from that you have concluded that this Ben Caviness is the person we are looking for?" the chief constable asked.

"Yes."

"Other than the fact that the woman in St. Louis was killed by having her throat cut, and the victims here were killed by having their throats cut, what possible connection can you make?" Dolan asked. "One event took place in St. Louis, which is at least a thousand miles from here, and the other events took place here in Philadelphia."

"There was also a similar event in Alexandria, Ohio," Preacher said.

"Where is Alexandria, Ohio?" Coleman asked.

"That is a town on the Ohio River, between here and St. Louis. There, two people, a husband and his wife, had their throats cut."

"And you think the person who killed the two people in Ohio is the same person you are looking for?"

"Yes, I know it is," Preacher replied.

"How do you know it is the same person?"

"Because there were witnesses to that murder. The two people who were killed were Mr. and Mrs. Potter. And their son and daughter saw the killer."

"Oh," the chief constable said. "Oh, my. Do you mean to tell me that those two children saw their own parents killed?"

"Yes. Well, they weren't children exactly. The boy was seventeen years old, and made a very credible witness. There is no doubt that the person he described as the killer is Ben Caviness."

The chief constable clucked, and shook his head. "What a shame they should have to witness such a thing," he said. "But how can you be certain that the man they described is the one you are looking for? I mean, just in a general description."

"This was more than a general description," Preacher explained. "Turns out that when Caviness attacked the woman in New York, her dog chewed off his ear."

"I'll be damned," the chief said. "So what you are telling me is that you have come to Philadelphia to look for a man with one ear, who also happens to be cutting down our citizens like a scythe through wheat."

"Yes," Preacher replied.

"All right, suppose I believe everything you are saying. And, God help me, I think I do believe you.

What makes you think that this Caviness person you are looking for is even in Philadelphia?"

"Because I think he has come here to extort money from Theodore Epson. He used to be a banker at the River Bank of St. Louis. But now he is with some bank here." Preacher went on to explain how Epson had stolen money from Jennie.

"And when Jennie started making trouble for him, I believe he hired Ben Caviness to kill her," he said, finishing the explanation.

"That is about the wildest story I've ever heard," Constable Coleman said. He looked at the chief constable. "Chief, I apologize for bringing him in here to see you. I thought he might have something, but he is really clutching at straws to put all that together and say that that we are looking for the same man."

"I'm not so sure, Coleman," the chief constable said. He drummed his fingers on the desk for a moment. "As crazy as it sounds, I think it might be exactly the way he says."

"So, what are we going to do? Start looking for a man with only one ear?" Coleman asked.

"Why not? At least it gives us something and someone to look for. That's better than chasing after a ghost."

"Yeah," Coleman said. "Yeah, I guess you do have a point there."

"I intend to search for him as well," Preacher said. He showed Dolan the letter that had been given to him by Constable Billings back in St. Louis.

Dolan looked at the letter for a moment. "Well,

I'm afraid this letter won't have much authority with any of our judges here."

"I see," Preacher said. He didn't react negatively to it because he had already made up his mind. With or without local permission, he was going to hunt Ben Caviness down, and he was going to make certain that justice was done.

"But," the chief constable continued, pulling out a piece of paper, "I can take care of that." He wrote something on the paper, then signed his name. "I'll make you my special deputy. This will give you authority to act in Philadelphia."

"Thank you," Preacher replied.

Epson had never seen or even heard of Preacher. But when he saw Preacher come into the Trust Bank of Philadelphia, he had a feeling about him. The man wearing buckskins was tall and muscular, like someone who lived and worked in the wilderness. He had seen several such men when he was in St. Louis. And if this man was from St. Louis, that couldn't be good.

He watched as the man spoke to someone, then, with a sinking feeling, watched the man approach his desk.

"Your name is Theodore Epson?" the man asked when he reached Epson.

"I am," Epson replied. "And you are?"

"Preacher."

"Preacher?"

"That's all you need to know. Epson, Jennie was

a friend of mine. In fact, she was a very special friend, if you get my meaning."

"Jennie?"

"Yes, Jennie. You will remember her, I'm sure. She is the young lady you stole nine hundred fifty dollars from."

"I did no such thing!"

"Sure you did," Preacher said easily. "Both Mr. Ashley and Jenny gave you the money to pay off her mortgage and you kept it."

"There are no signed papers anywhere that supports that claim," Epson said. "You would never be able to prove that in a court of justice."

Preacher chuckled ominously. "You don't understand, do you, Epson. I don't need to prove it. I only need to believe it. I'm the only justice you will ever see."

"What . . . what are you going to do?" Epson asked, his voice quivering in fear.

"Oh, I don't intend to do anything yet. You are my bait."

"Your bait?"

"I'm a fur trapper, Epson. I know that you don't catch your quarry without using bait. Right now, my quarry is the man who killed Jennie. Things didn't work out quite the way he thought they would, so it's my bet that he'll be looking you up. Since he's already in Philadelphia, all I have to do is keep an eye on you. Like I said, Epson, you are my bait."

"Ben Caviness is in Philadelphia?"

Preacher laughed dryly. "I didn't say anything about Ben Caviness."

At first, Epson thought he had been caught. Then he smiled as he remembered that Miller said Caviness was the murder suspect in Jennie's case.

"No, you didn't say anything about him, but Mr. Miller did. Mr. Miller just returned from St. Louis, and he told me about the tragic events surrounding Miss Jennie. And he said that Ben Caviness was the prime suspect, so naturally, when you said the murderer was in Philadelphia, I made the connection."

"Did you now?" Preacher asked.

"Yes. How else would I have known that you were talking about Ben Caviness?"

"I wonder," Preacher replied. "How else?"

"What makes you think Caviness is in Philadelphia?"

"As he passed through Ohio, on his way to Philadelphia, he killed a man and his wife by slitting their throats. There have been four killed here by having their throats slit. I believe the killer is Ben Caviness."

Involuntarily, Epson put his hand to his own throat. "What I don't understand is why you think he would want to look me up."

"Like I said, things didn't go well for him back in St. Louis. I think he's coming to see you in order to ask for more money."

"I'm . . . sure that I don't know what you talking about," Epson said, though his protest sounded weak even to his own ears.

\*\*\*

Caviness was sitting at a table with three others in the Bucket of Blood Tavern. He no longer resembled the man who had arrived in Philadelphia nearly six weeks ago. His hair had grown long enough to cover the missing ear. And with the money he took from the men he had killed, he'd bought clothes that were more in the style of the average Philadelphia citizen. Because he was now blending in with the others, he no longer drew curious stares from the casual observer. He was still rough-looking, but no more rough looking than the men who were sitting at the table with him.

To the degree that a person like Caviness could make friends, he had befriended these three. Several times over the last few days, he had encountered them here in the Bucket of Blood Tavern. Like Caviness, none of the three men seemed to have any visible source of income.

Caviness bought a round of beer for them. "I need to find me somebody," he said as he lifted the mug to his lips. "I don't reckon none of you know a feller by the name of Epson, do you?"

"I know a man named Epson," one of the men said. This was Jim Gray. "But he prob'ly ain't the one you're lookin' for."

"How do you know he's not?"

"'Cause he's one of them bigwigs that works in a bank."

"Yes!" Caviness said excitedly. This was his first real lead. "The fella I'm looking for works in a bank. It's got to be the same man. Where is the bank?"

Gray laughed. "Well, they's a lot more'n one

bank in Philadelphia," he said. "But the one Epson works in is the Trust Bank. What you need to see him for?"

"He owes me money," Caviness said.

Gray stroked his chin as he stared across the table at Caviness. "Does he now?" he asked.

"Yes."

"What's in it for me if I take you to him?"

"I'll give you a dollar," Caviness replied. He could afford to be generous. He planned to get a lot more than a dollar from Epson.

"Make it two dollars, and you got yourself a deal," Gray insisted.

"All right, two dollars. But for that, I want you to take me to him."

Gray finished his beer, then wiped the back of his hand across his mouth.

"You got yourself a deal," Gray said. "Let's go." He stood up.


Epson stepped out to the privy behind the bank. When he returned, he saw two men standing by his desk, but as there was nothing unusual about their looks or demeanor, he approached them without any sense of concern.

"Yes, gentlemen, may I help you?" Epson asked, greeting them with his practiced mile.

"Hello, Epson," Caviness said.

"Caviness!" Epson said. "What are you doing here?"

"I took care of that little job you had for me back in St. Louis," Caviness said.

"Shh," Epson said, looking around the bank to see if anyone was close enough to overhear them. "Who is this?" Epson asked, indicating Gray.

"This here is Jim Gray," Caviness said. "He's a pal of mine. Now, about that business in St. Louis."

Epson put his finger across his lips in a signal to be quiet. "Let's step outside to discuss this," he said. "I don't want everyone listening in to our business."

"All right," Caviness agreed.

"Mr. Sinclair, I'm going to step out front for a moment," Epson said to the chief teller.

"Very well, Mr. Epson," Sinclair replied.

The three men walked outside, then stood in front of the bank.

"What are you doing in Philadelphia?" Epson asked.

"I need more money," Caviness replied.

"I paid you a fair price," Epson said.

"Yeah, well, things didn't go the way I thought they would."

"Yes, I know, the dog chewed off your ear, but that's your problem, not mine."

Gray laughed. "That's what happened to you ear?" he said. "A dog chewed it off?"

"It ain't funny," Caviness said. He looked at Epson. "How did you know about my ear?"

"Preacher told me."

"Preacher?" Caviness's eyes grew wide. "Where did you see Preacher?"

"I saw him here in my office yesterday," Epson said.

"What the hell is he doing here?"

"He's after you, Caviness."

Caviness looked around, his face clearly reflecting his fear at the mention of Preacher's name.

"How did the son of a bitch know I was here?"

"He followed you here from St. Louis."

Gray laughed again. "What's got you so spooked?" he asked Caviness. "You that scared of a preacher?"

"He ain't a preacher," Caviness said. Then to Espon. "What did you tell him?"

"How could I tell him anything? I didn't even know you were in Philadelphia."

"This is bad. This is real bad."

Suddenly Epson got an idea. "Maybe not," he said. "Not if we're smart."

"You got an idea?"

"Yes," Epson said. "You want some more money?"

"Hell, yes, I do. I told you, that's why I'm here."

"All right. I'll pay you some more money." He looked at Gray. "And I'll pay you as well. All you have to do is take care of Preacher."

"What do you mean, 'take care of Preacher'?" Gray asked.

"What do you think I mean?"

"I think it means you want us to kill him," Gray said.

This was Epson's moment of truth. He had danced around being a thief, and he had danced around the responsibility for Jennie's death. But things had gone too far now. It was time to fish or cut bait, and the way he saw it, Preacher had left him no choice.

"Yes," Epson said. "I'll give you one hundred dollars apiece to kill him."

"One hundred dollars? Yeah, I'll do it. How hard can it be to kill a preacher?" Gray replied.

"I told you, he's not a preacher," Caviness said. "And he is going to be a hard man to kill. I've run into him before." Caviness looked at Epson. "A hundred dollars ain't enough. You give me one hundred dollars to take care of your problem in St. Louis. Taking care of your problem here is going to be even harder."

Epson smiled. "He's not just my problem," he said. "He's after you too. Think about it, Caviness. You are going to have to face him one way or the other. This way, at least, you are getting paid for it."

"A hundred dollars sounds good to me," Gray said.

"Make it one hundred and twenty dollars," Caviness said.

"Why one hundred and twenty?" Epson asked.

Caviness looked at Gray. "You think Scott and Kelly would throw in with us for ten dollars apiece?"

Gray laughed. "Yeah, if we don't tell 'em how much we're getting. But you really think we are going to need them?"

"I told you. This Preacher is one tough son of a bitch," Caviness said. "Yeah, we're going to need them." He looked back at Epson. "What about it, Epson? One hundred and twenty dollars apiece?"

"All right," he said. He held up his finger. "But not until the job is done."

"We've got to have some of the money now," Caviness said.

"I'll give you ten dollars apiece now, plus ten dollars for your two friends. Come back to me when the job is done, and I'll give you the rest."

"All right," Caviness agreed. "But try and hold out on me when I come back, and I'll slit your throat from ear to ear."

Epson shuddered. How had he ever let his life get so out of hand that he was in league with men like this?

"I won't cheat you," he promised.

# TWENTY

The lobby of the Federal Hotel had a red carpet and was dotted here and there with potted plants, chairs, and benches. Coming in off Fourth Street, the stairwell to the upper three floors was to the left of the lobby, while the registration desk was to the right.

When Preacher returned to the hotel from lunch, written in chalk on a slate just inside the door was a sign that read: MR. PREACHER TO THE DESK, PLEASE.

Preacher picked his way through the potted plants. The clerk was making entries in a ledger. He looked up as Preacher approached.

"I'm Preacher."

"Yes, this was delivered for you, sir," the clerk said, handing him an envelope.

"Thank you," Preacher said.

Preacher climbed the stairs to his room, then sat in the light of the window to examine the envelope. There was no name or address on the outside. He withdrew a one-page letter.

*Dear Preacher,*
*Shortly after you called upon me I was visited by Ben Caviness. I confess that I did ask*

*him to frighten Jennie, so she would stop making false claims against me. But I did not ask, nor did I expect, him to kill her.*

*Now, just as you said he would, he has asked me for more money. I told him that I would not give him any more money, and I took him to task for misinterpreting my instructions. He grew very angry and threatened to kill me if I did not comply with his demand for more money. Therefore, it is for my own safety that I tell you where to find him.*

*You will not find him staying in a hotel. Rather, he has made camp in the park area of Kensington, very near a place known as "Elephant Rock." It was in this same area that the first of our recent murders took place, and I am now convinced that Caviness was responsible for those terrible killings.*

*Therefore, were you to take care of him, you will not only achieve justice for yourself and your lady-friend, but peace of mind for the citizens of Philadelphia, who are now too frightened to leave their homes at night.*

*Theodore Epson*

Preacher did not believe for one moment that Epson's instructions to Caviness had been misunderstood. He was convinced that Epson had wanted Jennie killed.

He was equally convinced that this wasn't a letter giving up Caviness, but was, instead, a letter designed to set him up. He was certain that once he showed up at the park in Kensington, he would be ambushed by Ben Caviness. But as they say, forewarned is forearmed. Preacher intended to keep that rendezvous.

If Epson went so far as to set Preacher up for an ambush, then he was sure that the banker had even more surprises in store for him. Therefore, before Preacher left the hotel that night, he prepared himself for any eventuality. He had two pistols, loaded and stuck down into his belt. He also had two knives— one on his belt and one stuck down into his boot.

Thus armed, he entered the park.

There was no moon tonight, so it was very dark. Even more so because the park was some distance from the ambient light of the city. The night sky was alive with the sounds of insects and frogs, as well as the silent whisper of the Schuylkill River. Although he was in the middle of a great city, Preacher was more at home right now than he had been at any time since leaving the mountains. He was in the middle of a wilderness, albeit a small one, listening to the ebb and flow of the sounds and moving with—not intruding upon—the natural order of things.

As he approached Elephant Rock, he noticed something that not one other person in Philadelphia would have noticed. There was a slight disruption in the sound patterns made by the night creatures, and that disruption told him that someone was very close and watching him. The hackles stood up on the back of Preacher's neck and he eased one of his pistols from his belt, then cocked it.

Suddenly a shot was fired. The night was lit up by the light from the muzzle flash. In an instinctive reaction, Preacher had anticipated the shot by no more than an instant, and he dove to the right.

Hitting the ground, Preacher rolled quickly to his right, as the ball whizzed by where he had been but a moment before. Had he not moved when he did, he would be dead now.

Preacher returned fire, and was momentarily blinded by his own muzzle flash. In addition, tiny bits of expended gunpowder peppered his face. He heard a grunting sound, then the sound of someone falling.

Remaining on his belly, he crawled forward until he reached the body of the man he had just shot. Rolling him over, he saw that the man was dead.

He also saw that it wasn't Ben Caviness.

A second shot hit the rock just above Preacher, then careened off through the park, its transit marked by a whining sound.

"Scott, did you get him?" someone called. Preacher did not recognize the voice. "Scott, did you get him?" the voice repeated.

"Nah, the son of a bitch got Scott," another voice answered. "Scott is dead." Preacher didn't recognize this voice either. How many were out here?

"Kelly, Gray, quit your jabbering and wait for a shot," a third voice called from the darkness.

This voice, Preacher did recognize. It was Ben Caviness.

"Caviness," Preacher called. "I'm coming after you, Caviness."

"Come ahead, you son of a bitch!" Caviness shouted. His shout was punctuated with a pistol shot, and once again a ball passed dangerously close.

Preacher returned fire, and saw his bullet strike sparks as it hit a rock. He also heard Caviness yelp in pain, though he knew that hadn't done any real damage to the outlaw. The best he could have done was to send shards of his bullet into him. That would be painful, but certainly not fatal.

"Kelly, he's already fired twice," Gray called. "Unless he's carryin' a whole bag of guns, he's got nothin' left."

"Let's get 'im!" Kelly yelled.

Suddenly, two men jumped up from their place of concealment, no more than thirty feet in front of Preacher. With shouts of defiance, they rushed toward him, their pistols leveled.

Preacher filled his hands with his two knives. He waited until they had closed to within ten feet, then suddenly stood up in front of them.

"There he is!" Gray shouted.

Gray and Kelly fired simultaneously while, at the same time, Preacher brought both his arms forward, throwing the two knives. The dual muzzle flashes momentarily illuminated the park. In a picture that was frozen in time, the two knives seemed to hang in the air, the points of the blades toward Kelly and Gray, suspended between Preacher and his two adversaries

The two assailants saw the knives coming toward them, but they had no time for any reaction other than fear. Both blades struck the men in the chests, burying deep. With groans of pain, they went down.

By now, the two bullets they had fired were landing harmlessly in the river beyond.

Now Preacher was effectively unarmed. Both pistols were empty, both knives expended. He dropped behind a rock, then moved quickly and silently to his left in order to reload.

His own pistol empty, Caviness left after his brief exchange with Preacher. He was already on his way out of the park when he heard Kelly and Gray's challenge. He also heard the discharge of their weapons. What he did not hear was their shouts of victory, and had they killed Preacher, he knew they would have let it be known.

The silence could only mean that they missed, or even more likely, that somehow Preacher had killed them. And Caviness believed it was the latter. He knew Preacher, had run across him before, and he knew what the man was capable of.

Caviness had only one thought in mind now, and that was to find Epson, get his money, and get out of Philadelphia.

The only way Caviness knew how to find Epson was to return to the bank and stay there all night long. When Epson showed up for work the next morning, Caviness would be waiting for him.

It was daylight when Epson stepped down from the omnibus in front of the bank. Caviness was waiting behind a flowering shrub as Epson, nattily dressed in a suit, vest, and hat, came walking by. When he drew even with him, Caviness suddenly stepped out into the path in front of him.

Epson gasped, then took a step back. "Caviness!" he said. "What are you doing here?"

Caviness looked awful. His face was cut and swollen where the shards of Preacher's bullet had cut into him. He smiled, showing stained, crooked, and broken teeth.

"Well, now, is that any way to greet an old pal?" he asked.

"We aren't . . . pals," Epson said.

Caviness put his hand over his heart. "Well, now, that pains me deeply, that you don't consider us pards," he said. The smile left. "But that makes no never mind. Just give me my two hundred dollars, and I'll be on my way."

"Did you . . . that is—is Preacher dead?"

"No, Preacher ain't dead," Caviness said. "But all my pards is. You're hard luck to be around, you know that, Epson? First off, Slater gets hisself kilt back in St. Louis and I get my ear chewed off. Then my new pards that I met here got themselves kilt last night. Three of 'em," he added. "They was three of them and one of me, so that we was four to one against Preacher. But that didn't make no never mind. He kilt all three of them."

"Four of you against one man, and he got away?"

"Yeah. So you can see, Epson, the best thing for me to do is just get the hell out of Philadelphia, only I can't do that if I ain't got no money. So, I'll take that two hundred dollars you was goin' to give me."

"That money was to be disbursed only if you killed Preacher," Epson said.

Caviness pulled his pistol. "Yeah, well, I didn't kill him, but you are going to *disburse* it anyway," he said mockingly.


Even before sunrise, Preacher was pretty sure that Caviness had gotten away from him somehow, sneaking out of the park under the cover of darkness. He dragged the bodies of the three men he had killed into a spot that was some distance from the normal path people took when walking through the park. With the bodies out of the way of incidental pedestrians, he went to the headquarters of the Philadelphia Police Agency to report upon the events of the night before.

Chief Constable Dolan, Constable Coleman, and a couple of the watchmen, including one whose "watch box" was very near the entrance of the park, were there to, listen as Preacher told his story.

"You think it happened the way this man says it happened?" Constable Coleman asked after Preacher was finished.

"Why? Do you think it didn't?"

"I don't know . . . four men against one, and this morning three of the four is dead. It don't ring right to me."

Dolan nodded. "Well, I believe it," he said. "Let's go down to the park and have a look."

Accepting a ride in Dolan's carriage, Preacher led them into the park and to the place where he had left the bodies this morning. They were still there, undisturbed.

Chief Dolan looked at them for a moment, then pointed out the bodies, identifying them one by one. "That's Jim Gray, Luke Kelly, and Martin Scott," he said. "They are the dregs of society, three of the most disreputable men in the city. If they were out here in the park in the middle of the night, you can bet they were up to no good. Preacher did the whole city a favor by killing these three."

"Thanks," Preacher said. "But the one I wanted got away."

At that moment, a constable on horseback came riding into the park at a gallop.

"Chief!" he started shouting, even before he dismounted. Dismounting, he handed the reins of his horse to one of the other watchmen, then hurried over to Chief Constable Dolan.

"What is it, Smith?"

"Some banker has been taken prisoner," Smith said.

"Taken prisoner? What do you mean 'taken prisoner'?"

"A fella by the name of Epson," Smith said. "Witnesses say another man jumped out from behind some bushes this morning and took him at gunpoint down to the river."

"Epson?" Preacher said. "Chief Dolan, if Epson has been taken prisoner, then Caviness has to be the one who took him."

The recently arrived watchman looked at the tall man in buckskins, then looked back at Dolan. "Who is this?"

"This is my deputy," Dolan said. "Come on, let's get down to the river."

Down at the river's edge, Caviness had commandeered a small paddle boat. Ordering the boatman to build up the steam, he stood there, pointing his pistol at Epson, while a crowd of curious onlookers began gathering around to watch the unfolding drama.

"My name is Constable Marvin Jensen," one of the men in the crowd shouted to Caviness. This was a watchman, a member of the Philadelphia Police whose watchbox was close enough to the area to arouse his interest in what was going on by the river. He'd arrived to find Caviness standing there by the edge of the water, holding a pistol pointed at the head of a very frightened Theodore Epson. "Just what is it you are planning on doing?" the constable asked.

"I'm going to kill him if anyone comes any closer," Caviness replied with a menacing jerk of his gun.

"You don't want to do that, mister. That would be cold-blooded murder, and you would hang for it for sure," the watchman replied.

"You want to save this man's life?" Caviness called.

"Yes."

"Then you go to this here feller's bank, and you

tell the person in charge there that he had better come up with two hundred—no, make that one thousand dollars. Yeah, one thousand," he repeated, getting bolder. "You tell the bank it's going to cost them one thousand dollars to keep me from killin' this here little pissant."

"What makes you think the bank will pay one thousand dollars to save this man?" the constable asked.

" 'Cause he ain't just anybody. This here feller works for that bank. I reckon they'll pay to save him," Caviness said with self-assurance.

"Caviness, Mr. Fontaine is never going to agree to something like that," Epson said in a voice that was laced with panic. "He won't pay one thousand, he won't pay one dollar."

"Then you're going to die," Caviness replied. He looked toward the boatman. "How much longer before we have steam?" he demanded.

"Not much longer," the boatman replied.

"Hurry it up," Caviness said.

"You can't make steam any faster than you can make steam," the boatman complained.

While holding the gun in one hand, Caviness pulled his knife with the other. "You'd better figure out some way to do it," he said. "Or I'll split you open like guttin' a fish."

"No, no, it won't be much longer," the boatman promised.

"It better not be," Caviness said. Then he turned to Epson. "The bank has got until this here feller gets the steam built up to come down here with my one thousand dollars," he said.

"What if . . . what if they don't get here before the steam is up?" Epson asked in a frightened voice.

"Then you'll be leaving with me. Leastwise, till I figure out what to do with you."

The drama continued to play out on the banks of the Schuylkill River, the boatman working hard to build up the steam while an ever-growing crowd gathered to see what was going on. Now and then someone would yell at Caviness, imploring him to release Epson, but Caviness paid no attention to them and, eventually, the crowd became still.

The situation became very eerie as hundreds of people stared in silence at the three men who were standing on the small paddle boat.

Finally the boatman spoke.

"Steam's up," he said.

"All right. Let's go," Caviness ordered.

"Go where?" the boatman asked.

"Downriver," Caviness replied. "As fast as you can make this thing go."

"Wait!" Epson shouted.

"Wait for what?"

"The bank. You haven't given them enough time to bring the money to you."

Caviness laughed an evil laugh. "They ain't goin' to bring me no money," he said. "You done told me that yourself."

At that moment, a carriage arrived at the river's edge, its team pulling it at a gallop. Three men got out of the carriage. Caviness didn't recognize two of them, but he did recognize the third. It was Preacher. Damn, the son of a bitch did get away last night.

"Hurry up! Let's go!" Caviness shouted to the boatman. Seeing Preacher this close put Caviness on edge. "Come on, let's get out of here!"

The boatman cast off, then opened the throttle. The paddles slapped at the water, and the little boat moved quickly out into the stream.

As the space between the boat and the river's edge widened, Caviness began feeling more and more secure. He was going to get away after all. He felt emboldened.

"Hey, Preacher!" Caviness called out to him in a challenging tone of voice. "What are you going to do now, huh?" He laughed wickedly. "Are you going to keep chasing me?"

"Until I catch you," Preacher answered.

"Yeah, well, you better give it up. You're getting too many people killed," Caviness said. "Your woman in St. Louis, them two back in Ohio, the ones here. I kilt them all, but you're to blame for it, Preacher. You're the blame 'cause you're chasin' me, and as long as you keep comin' after me, the more killin' I'm going to do."

"Did you hear that, Chief?" Coleman asked. "That man just admitted to being the murderer we've been looking for."

"Yes, I heard."

"Well, what are we going to do about it? He's getting away."

"There's nothing we can do, right now," Dolan said.

By now the boat was mid-river and making its way downstream. With the brisk current and full power, the little boat was moving much faster than a horse could gallop.

Suddenly, the three men saw a flash of smoke, then heard a pop. Epson fell into the water.

"Holy shit! He just killed Epson!" Coleman said as the crowd gasped at the horror of what they had just seen.

Glancing back toward the carriage, Preacher saw that there was a rifle in the carriage boot. He walked over to it, picked it up, and examined it for a moment. Then he began loading it. Glancing back toward the carriage, the chief constable saw Preacher with the rifle.

"What are you doing?" he asked.

"I don't intend to just stand by and let him get away from me this time," Preacher said as he reached for the powder horn and pouch of balls.

"Are you joking? He's already out of range. By the time you get that rifle loaded, he'll be well out of range."

"Maybe," Preacher said as he poured powder into the rifle. "But I aim to try."

Out on the boat, which was now some distance from shore, Caviness stood on top of the cabin, looking back toward the landing. The figures were growing smaller as the distance widened, and Caviness laughed.

"I beat you, you son of a bitch!" he shouted. "I beat you!"

That was when he saw Preacher come down to the water's edge, kneel, and aim a rifle at him.

"Ha! What do you think you are doing?" Caviness shouted. "Why, you ignorant bastard! You are so far . . ."

Caviness saw a flash of light and a puff of smoke. He saw Preacher rock back from the recoil.

" . . . out of range . . . unnh!"

Caviness felt a hammerlike blow, as if he had been kicked by a mule. It knocked him back a step and he put his hand up to his chest, then watched in horror and disbelief as his cupped palm filled with blood.

"Well, I'll be damned," Caviness said just as the world around him began to fade. He pitched forward into the river and floated, facedown very still.

*The Rocky Mountains*

When Preacher reached the top of the summit, he stood there for a moment. Gazing down on the vista, he saw an endless slope of mottled treetops—from various shades of green, to golden aspen, to crimson. Across a rolling basin, there was a wall of red rock, broken along its face into points, ledges, cliffs, and escarpments.

An early fall snow had already crowned Eagle's

Beak, and once again, Preacher saw feathery tendrils of snow streaming out from it. The crystals glistened in the sun, forming a prism of color that crowned the beauty of the scene.

How different this was from Philadelphia, St. Louis, or even Kansas City. There, amidst the buildings and the clatter of traffic and the crowd of people, he had been totally out of his element. Even while visiting his family—though he was pleased to see them after so many years, and happy that his brother and sisters were doing well—he had felt a nagging discontent, a need to get back where he belonged.

Overhead, an eagle soared, and just before him, Preacher could hear the sound of a babbling creek. He got a whiff of the sweet smell of pine and caught the musk of distant forest animals.

"What do you think, Dog?" he asked the animal who had been keeping pace with him as they traveled higher and higher into the mountains. "Are you happy to be home?"

Dog looked up at him.

"I almost left you with Cara, you know. She begged me to. But I figure, with that restaurant I bought her, she doesn't need a dog around. Besides, I missed you," he said. "Why, if I didn't have you to talk to, folks would think I'm talking to myself."

The mountain man laughed loudly at his own joke, his laughter echoing back from the woods.

Don't miss
NO MAN'S LAND,
next in the Last Gunfighter series
now available from Pinnacle Books.


For a sneak preview, just turn the page . . .

Frank heard the wagons coming long before they actually came into view. Five big fine wagons, looking brand-spanking-new to Frank. Big prairie schooners, each one pulled by six of the finest mules Frank had seen in a long time. Big red Missouri mules. A single scout, or wagon master, rode about a hundred yards in front of the wagons. There were five other mounted men, three on one side of the wagons, two on the other, the men all carrying rifles.

Frank sat on the ridge overlooking what passed for a trail, and watched the slow procession of the wagon train. When the trail boss drew within hailing distance, Frank lifted the reins and rode down to intercept him.

The scout spotted Frank and lifted his arms, halting the train. His hand dropped to the butt of his pistol.

"No need for that, friend," Frank called. "I mean you no harm."

"State your business," the scout called.

"Some company on the trail. Maybe some coffee when you decide to make camp for the evening."

"You alone?"

"I am what you see."

"Look at the pretty dog, Mama!" a girl called from a wagon, pointing at Dog.

"Does he bite, mister?" another girl called from another wagon.

Dog sat on his haunches beside Stormy, not moving.

"Only if you try to do him harm," Frank called.

"I'm been looking for a place to camp," the scout said. You know this country?"

"I do not. I've been heading east for the past week, but staying out of the strip."

"We're just north of the strip, I think."

"Yes. About ten miles."

"You have a name?"

Frank smiled. "Frank Morgan."

The trail master was visibly shaken at that. When he found his voice, he shouted, *"Frank Morgan!"*

That got everyone's attention. Those in the wagons nearest Frank and the trail boss sat and stared in silence at the mention of the West's most famous gunfighter.

"I'm not on the prod for anyone," Frank told the trailboss. "I'm just drifting, seeing the country."

"You're welcome to ride along with us, Mr. Morgan." The man held out a hand. "I'm Steve Wilson."

Frank took the friendship hand, and the two men

took the point, the heavy wagons lumbering along
behind them.

"Fine-looking wagons," Frank remarked.

"Aren't they, though. All of them special built
in Indiana for this trip. And we're almost home."

"Oh?"

"Colorado. In another week or so, we'll turn
some north and then it's on to home."

"Farmers?"

"You bet. And we're all good farmers too. It's
just getting too crowded back in Indiana. We all
wanted some space to stretch out some."

"I sure know that feeling."

"That's a fine-looking horse you're riding, Mr.
Morgan. I don't believe I ever seen one quite like
it."

"Appaloosa, Mr. Wilson. Nez Percé Indians
breed them."

"Beautiful animal. Very striking."

They rode on for a few hundred yards without
speaking, only the creaking of the big wagons
breaking the silence. Topping a small rise, Frank
pointed.

"Looks like a little creek down there, Mr. Wilson. Might be a good spot to camp for the night."

"Looks good to me, too, Mr. Morgan. I'll ride
back and tell the others."

"Before you do, Mr. Wilson, I'd like to make a
suggestion."

"Certainly."

"Let's drop the 'mister' business before we wear

each other out. I'm Frank and you're Steve. How about it?"

The wagon master laughed. "Sounds good to me, Frank. Deal."

Frank smiled. "I'll check out the camp area."

Frank squatted by the creek and watched as Steve positioned the wagons in a tight circle. The man knew his business, Frank thought. No doubt about that.

Water was drawn from the creek for cooking and drinking and filling of barrels; then the mules and horses were led down to drink. Frank helped gather firewood for cooking, ignoring the surprised looks he received from the men for doing so. The women thanked him softly and the kids followed him around, the young boys trying to emulate Frank's walk.

The stock was settled in for the night, firewood was gathered, cook fires were going, camp ovens were out, and the women were busy mixing and stirring and kneading. The men all got themselves cups of fresh-brewed coffee and settled down for some conservation.

Frank was introduced to the men: Able Brandon, he was married to Carolyn. They had three kids, two girls and a boy. Weldon Freeman, his wife was Paula. They had three kids, two boys and a girl. Randall Fossmon, he was married to Judith. They were the oldest couple there. They had four kids, all in their teens, two boys, two girls. Harry Ellington, married to Betty. Two kids, a boy and a girl. And Virgil Carpenter. His wife's name was Dixie. They had three kids, two girls, one boy.

"My mother liked the name," Dixie explained.

"I call her by her middle name," Virgil said. "Lou."

"I'll call you Dixie," Frank said, taking the woman's small hand into his big callused hand.

The very attractive woman flushed just a bit, and Frank quickly released her hand. Her husband seemed not to notice. Never did like that name," Virgil said. "I guess it came from my time in the war. I fought against the Rebs. I was a boy really. But I killed my share of them damn stinkin' Rebs. Did you fight in the war, Morgan?"

"Yes, I did," Frank replied, and said no more about it. He looked at Able Branson. "You all have some fine-looking mules, Able. Are they plow broke?"

"I wouldn't know, sir," Able replied. Frank picked up on the sly look in the man's eyes.

"We'll be honest with you, Frank." Steve said. "We tell everyone we're going out to farm. But we're really not."

"Steve . . . " Weldon Freeman said, a note of caution in his voice.

"Oh, it's all right," the wagon boss said. "I know bit more about Morgan than you folks. I read a long article about him in the St.Louis paper. Mr. Morgan is a rich man. Isn't that right, Frank?"

Frank nodded his head. "I reckon I'm worth considerable, for a fact."

"But you're just drifting around," Betty Ellington remarked. "Don't you have a real home?"

Frank smiled. "I have all this," he said, waving a hand at the sky and the land around him.

"But don't you want more?" Judith asked.

"I have a nice home in the mountains west of here." Frank replied. "I'll retire there someday. Raise cattle and horses. But that is years down the road."

"So for now you just . . . drift around?" Dixie asked.

"I enjoy life," Frank replied.

"And take life occasionally, so I hear," Randall said, but without any detectable note of malice in the statement.

"If I'm pushed," Frank said. He turned his gaze to Steve. "So if you're not going to farm in Colorado, what are you people going to do?"

"Hunt for gold," Steve replied, his voice almost a whisper.

"Gold?" Frank asked.

"Yes, sir," Able said. "In the Sangre de Cristo Mountains. That's west of Canon City. So far only a few people know about it. We're going to be among the first to stake our claims."

"It's also Ute country," Frank reminded them.

"Oh," Steve said, waving a hand, "I was told the Utes are no longer much of a problem. Besides, these good folks are not looking to get rich. Just enough of a stake for them to start businesses in the town itself."

"I see," Frank replied. Something wasn't ringing true with Steve's remarks, but Frank let his suspicions slide for the moment. Frank sat quietly and drank his coffee, listening to the others talk while supper cooked. It was evident that they all held Steve in very high regard. Frank sure would have liked to have more information about Steve Wilson, but there wasn't a town with a telegraph within a three days' hard ride.

"I know a way that will cut days off your trip," Frank said. "That is, if you're interested."

"Oh, I think not," Steve said very quickly. Too quickly to suit Frank. "I know this way, and I think it would be best to stick with the planned route."

"Well, that might be best," Frank replied. "It was just a thought. Say, this is really good coffee. Mind if I have another cup?"

"Certainly, Mr. Morgan," Dixie said, leaning forward to take his cup and refill it from the big camp pot. "Here you are."

Frank smiled at her. "Much obliged, ma'am. I am a coffee-drinkin' man, for a fact."

With the sun low in the late afternoon sky, Dixie had taken off her bonnet, her honey-blond hair framing her face. Really a very lovely woman, Frank thought. Very shapely, with blond hair and blue eyes, but with a certain degree of sadness in her eyes. Frank wondered about that. Then, after a quick glance at her sour-faced husband, Frank ceased to wonder. He had yet to see the man smile.

Frank leaned back against a pile of boxes and listened to the travelers talk. But he was very conscious of Dixie's eyes occasionally touching him. Frank tried to avoid her gaze, but he was not always successful. There were curious questions in her eyes, and a number of silent promises.

"Don't mess with another man's wife," he thought. "It only leads to trouble."

"You plan on riding along with us for a ways, Morgan?" Able Branson asked.

"No," Frank replied. "I think I'll pull out come the morning. But I want to warn you folks to stay out of the strip just south of us. It's a mean place, filled with all sorts of trouble."

"Don't you worry about that, Frank," Steve said quickly. "I'll keep us out of no-man's-land."

"I thought you were going to ride with us for a time, Mr. Morgan," Paula said.

"Oh, I changed my mind, Mrs. Freeman," Frank said with a smile. "That's the nice thing about riding alone. A man can shift directions like the wind." Frank cut his eyes to Steve. The man looked relieved at the news of Frank's pulling out.

Something is definitely wrong here, Frank thought. Very wrong.

The next morning, several hours before dawn, as Frank was rolling up his blankets, Dixie slipped quietly through early morning mist to where Frank had camped.

"Mrs. Carpenter," Frank said. "You're up very early."

"I brought you a cup of coffee, Mr. Morgan. It's strong. Warmed up from last night."

"Thank you, ma'am. I appreciate it." Frank sipped the strong brew and met the woman's eyes in the darkness. "Something on your mind, Mrs. Carpenter?"

"I don't trust Mr. Wilson," the woman said bluntly.

"What does your husband think about him?"

"Oh, he thinks the man hung the moon and the stars."

Frank said nothing of his own reservations about Steve. "What's made you so suspicious of Steve?"

Dixie hesitated for a few seconds. "He's . . . well, devious, Mr. Morgan."

"Devious how?"

"When I asked him about all the other groups he's guided West, he gets very defensive, almost surly. Then he gets . . . oily is the best word I can think of to call it."

"But he won't give you a straight answer about the others?"

"No. Says he doesn't know what happened to them. Says they're spread out all over the West and that's all he'll say."

"Spread out may be true, Dixie."

"I know. But I still don't trust him. We're carrying a lot of money, Mr. Morgan. All of us. We sold everything we had before we left home, and many of us had money in the bank. And I'm not ashamed to admit, I'm scared something is going to happen."

Before Frank could reply, Steve Wilson's voice cut through the early morning air. "Fooling around with another man's wife can get a body dead out here, Morgan."

Frank turned to face the voice. "Nobody is fooling around with another man's wife, Wilson. Mrs. Carpenter was kind enough to bring me a cup of coffee before I pulled out."

"Then I beg your pardon . . . from both of you. I was wrong assuming the worst."

Dixie held out a small hand. "I'm glad we met, Mr. Morgan. I hope you eventually find what you're seeking."

Frank gently took the hand. "Thank you, Mrs. Carpenter. You and the others have a safe journey."

Frank released her hand, and Dixie was gone into the early morning darkness.

"So you're pulling out, Morgan?" Steve said.

"Right now, Wilson."

"Maybe we'll meet again."

"Count on it Wilson."

"What does that mean?"

"Means we're heading in the same direction, but taking different trails to get there."

Without another word, Wilson turned and walked away. Frank finished his coffee and set the empty cup on a wagon tongue.

"I just don't trust that fellow," Frank thought. "Something about him makes the hair on the back of my neck stand up."

Frank looked down at Dog, sitting on the ground, looking up at him. "You ready for the trail, ol' boy?"

Dog growled low in his throat.

"All right, boy, let's travel."

## THE LAST GUNFIGHTER SERIES BY
# WILLIAM W. JOHNSTONE

*Available Wherever Books Are Sold!*

Visit our website at **www.kensingtonbooks.com**

# THE EAGLES SERIES BY
# WILLIAM W. JOHNSTONE

__Eyes of Eagles
0-7860-1364-8                              **$5.99**US/**$7.99**CAN

__Dreams of Eagles
0-7860-6086-6                              **$5.99**US/**$7.99**CAN

__Talons of Eagles
0-7860-0249-2                              **$5.99**US/**$6.99**CAN

__Scream of Eagles
0-7860-0447-9                              **$5.99**US/**$7.50**CAN

__Rage of Eagles
0-7860-0507-6                              **$5.99**US/**$7.99**CAN

__Song of Eagles
0-7860-1012-6                              **$5.99**US/**$7.99**CAN

__Cry of Eagles
0-7860-1024-X                              **$5.99**US/**$7.99**CAN

__Blood of Eagles
0-7860-1106-8                              **$5.99**US/**$7.99**CAN

*Available Wherever Books Are Sold!*

Visit our website at **www.kensingtonbooks.com**

# BOOK YOUR PLACE ON OUR WEBSITE AND MAKE THE READING CONNECTION!

We've created a customized website just for our very special readers, where you can get the inside scoop on everything that's going on with Zebra, Pinnacle and Kensington books.

When you come online, you'll have the exciting opportunity to:

- View covers of upcoming books
- Read sample chapters
- Learn about our future publishing schedule (listed by publication month *and author*)
- Find out when your favorite authors will be visiting a city near you
- Search for and order backlist books from our online catalog
- Check out author bios and background information
- Send e-mail to your favorite authors
- Meet the Kensington staff online
- Join us in weekly chats with authors, readers and other guests
- Get writing guidelines
- AND MUCH MORE!

**Visit our website at
http://www.kensingtonbooks.com**